FAERY

WOlfMOON BOOK IV

NIKKI BROADWELL

Airmid Pubishing

Tucson, Arizona

Faery
Copyright © 2016. Nikki Broadwell

This is a work of fiction. All names, characters, places, and ideas presented here are a product of the author's imagination.

Formatting by: perryelisabethdesign.com

ISBN-10: 0-9979941-3-4

ISBN-13: 978-0-9979941-3-1

ACKNOWLEDGMENTS

Thank you to the muse who continues to sit on my shoulder and help me along.

Faeries, come take me out of this dull world,
For I would ride with you upon the wind,
Run on the top of the disheveled tide,
And dance upon the mountains like a flame.
~William Butler Yeats~
"The land of Heart's Desire"
1894

Chapter One

I was watching the moonrise over the hills to the east when I felt a hand come down on my shoulder.

"You should eat," Harold said quietly.

When I looked up his face looked blue in the shadows cast by the forest, the moon's silvery light giving his skin an eerie glow. He was my closest friend, my lover and the person who had accompanied me through the long days of war seven months before. We had been mentioned in the same prophecy and were destined to be together, here, now, in Otherworld.

"I'm not hungry."

"The baby needs food even if you think you don't," he said, a worried edge to his voice.

I let out a long sigh. It seemed like years that I'd been pregnant, my body's changes becoming more and more pronounced. I had odd cravings at odd times, my normal sleep and eating rhythms gone. My back ached nearly all the time—it couldn't be too much longer, could it? Rea had not been able to answer my questions that should have been posed to a doctor, and now that the Crion woman was also carrying a baby it seemed presumptuous to be pestering her about silly details. The baby would come when it was time—that was always Rea's answer and one I knew I should accept. This was not my modern world with answers at my fingertips on the nearest computer monitor.

The bonfires had been started, the flames crackling and spitting as they reached for the darkening sky. It was the night of Lughnasa, the ceremony to honor Lugh, the god of light, and to beg for a good harvest in six weeks time. My protector druid, MacCuill, was in process of lighting a fire, his fingers emitting blue flame as he walked slowly around the steeple of dried pine. The tribe known as the Crion, and the 'keepers of the wisdom' here in Otherworld, swayed around another fire already burning, their triangular faces lifted in silent adulation toward the sky. A distance away the heavy troll-like Oillteil, and the Wildmen, their brown hair matted into dreadlocks, chattered and laughed, their disparate languages melding into an interwoven fabric of sound. From where I sat on a hillock of thick grass I could watch the moon goddess move from one group to another, her mane of golden hair shimmering down her back in the moonlight, her gossamer silver dress shifting with each graceful step she took. Her lovely face glowed as though part of the moon, her eyes bright as she bent to bless each person.

After the years of cold and desolation in Otherworld, the prodigious growth of crops, flowers, grass and fruit trees had been a welcome surprise. Pregnancies had also abounded and barren women sure they would never conceive now carried babies. Even my faithful wolf, Finiche, had taken himself off to find a wolf mate and raise pups. I missed him but knew he would come back when the pups were old enough to travel. Watching the happiness all around I was struck again with how powerful the changes had been.

Unlike the people here, my baby had been conceived before I arrived in Otherworld, Harold's and my unprotected sex coming back to haunt us. We'd been friends for years, had gone to college together, but our intimate relationship had only begun a couple of months before I came to Scotland to visit my mother. The passion ignited between us had been a surprise, making us lose ourselves in the thrill of the moment. I'd been hard on my way to becoming the force to save Otherworld when I discovered the truth, and had to decide whether to keep it or find some way to abort; Rea knew of herbs that would have done the trick. But she was against it, and in the end convinced me as well. Considering the deprivation I'd put my body through during the early days it was a wonder the pregnancy had stuck.

Since the end of my great-uncle, Brandubh's, stranglehold on Otherworld, life had taken on a serenity that seemed almost too good to be true. But lately there was something at the back of my mind, a nagging feeling teasing its way forward hinting that contrary to appearances, all was not quite as it should be. Maybe it was the rise in hormones, or maybe it was because I could sense things here in Otherworld, things that might not have happened yet. These special gifts had become part of me, arriving full-blown in the first weeks after my unexpected arrival in Otherworld. I had been named in a prophecy, and although I hadn't believed it at first, the events that followed convinced me.

When I felt a kick my thoughts scattered like so many dried leaves, my hand going to my belly. Was she coming tonight? Arriving on Lughnasa would certainly be an auspicious beginning. But was I ready? A frisson of nerves went through me as I contemplated the enormity of taking care of a baby, especially in a place like this that had no amenities whatsoever. It had only been in the past year that several inns had been built, but the plumbing, if there was any, was rudimentary at best. Running water came from hollowed out logs and was gravity fed, cooking was done over fires, and as far as electricity, there was none.

"Maeve? Did you hear me?"

I brought my attention back to the dark-haired man standing next to me. "Sorry, Harold. I was caught up in the scene here and thinking about the birth." That was true enough, but eventually I would have to share my uneasiness with the man whose place here in Otherworld was as important as my own.

Harold took hold of my hand and pulled me up. "Time for Rea to take a look at you. If I had to predict I'd say this baby will be born sooner rather than later."

I laughed, letting go of my worry as he pulled me into his arms. "And I can't wait to see her," he whispered, his lips against my ear.

After Rea had plied me with a bit of mulled wine, she handed me a piece of fruit that resembled a pink pear/apple. "According to the moon goddess this one is particularly good for the baby," she told me. "Arianrhod brought it from her botanical garden especially for you."

I bit into the succulent rosy flesh, letting the juice drip down my chin. "It tastes like the moon."

"And what does the moon taste like, milady?"

I swatted at Harold but he moved out of the way, his chuckle making me laugh. Harold had discovered early on that one of his previous lives had been as the first king of Scotland. Even after the war was over he hung on to this persona. He still wore Kenneth McAlpin's sword on his hip, his face occasionally shifting into the more rugged features of the early king. The first king of Scotland's personality had served Harold well during the conflict, giving him a warrior's understanding of what was happening and how to use those skills. But I wondered why he still wore it—did he feel the same unease I did?

A sharp pain moved through my belly, cutting my thoughts off mid-stream. And a second later I was doubled over, trying to suppress the scream that threatened to rush out. I looked at what remained of the fruit in my hand, noticing the womb-like shape and the pinkish flesh. This was what had begun my labor.

"Maeve?" Harold bent over me, his brow furrowed.

"The fruit worked--the baby's coming," I managed to mutter just before another spasm shot through me.

Harold yelled for MacCuill and the two of them helped me toward the forest where Rea and the other Crion men and women had set up camp. Rea pointed us toward a small tent set apart that I was sure she'd prepared for just this eventuality. Sturdy poles in a teepee shape were covered in soft woven muslin, the same material as the dress Rea had given me when my clothing no longer fit.

Rea bustled around before taking my arm and leading me into the protected space. Rea had known exactly when my labor would come on and had helped it along with the fruit. When I asked her she said, "I knew it would be tonight. The fruit will make things go faster." When Harold tried to follow she shook her head no and pressed him firmly away. "This is women's work," the diminutive woman told him. "Once the baby comes you can join her."

"But…"

The curtain fell in his face just before I let out another piercing shriek.

As the hours went by I was aware of little other than pain and the murmuring and purring of the Crion who surrounded me. I felt their healing hands moving across my overheated skin, their voices soft and soothing, the smell of clary sage and other aromatic herbs burning on the fire filling my senses. I had been stripped of my clothes and now lay naked on a soft pallet beneath a light covering of woven material, a candle burning close by. One woman rubbed my feet, another rubbed my temples, as the labor went on and on. At some point they pulled me up so that I could crouch, telling me it was easier this way.

"The Willow must push now," I heard Rea say after another excruciating spasm that seemed never-ending. "She is ready to come out."

When the next contraction came I let out a scream that I was sure every person in Otherworld could hear, encouraged by the woman who kneeled between my legs. "Good," I heard Rea say through my miasma of pain. "Keep going." It seemed like hours of this, my energy ebbing as I attempted to do what Rea told me to do. Nothing had prepared me for this. When at last I felt something give and then the whoosh as the baby came, I fell back exhausted. The Crion women gathered the

12

baby up, one of them cutting the cord before another washed her gently from head to toe with sweet smelling water from a hollowed out gourd. A moment later the baby was swaddled in muslin and placed in my arms. So far she hadn't made a sound.

"Why hasn't she cried?" I asked worriedly.

Rea looked puzzled. "Why would she cry?"

"I thought all babies—" But the sentence was left unfinished as I peeled back the soft cloth to get a look at her. Harold and I had already named her Airmid after the goddess of the spring that brought the dead back to life. The goddess had saved each of our lives in her own way, her only stipulation that we name our baby after her. Baby Airmid's hair was a frizz of red, the same color as my thick curls, her eyes dark and knowing as she stared up at me. I couldn't stop the hot tears that flowed down my cheeks.

A second later the door flap opened and Harold rushed in, his face creased with worry. He kneeled on the ground next to the pallet. I smiled up at him and opened the blanket to show off our baby, my heart filled with more love than it could hold. And then Harold was bent over me, his own tears mingling with mine.

My mother arrived the next day to help me through the adjustment. And I was glad of it. "How did you even know the baby was here?" I asked her.

Finna lifted Airy out of my arms. "MacCuill sent a runner to let me know."

Rea's words rang in my ears: "You need to rest. Let your mother help with baby Airmid."

"My mother isn't here," I'd answered.

"She soon will be."

It seemed that everyone in Otherworld had magic; even my mother, who lived outside of this parallel world, must have left Bailemuir three days ago to get here in time.

For those first few days I seemed to fall asleep at a moment's notice. The time went by in dream-like fashion as I woke and slept and woke again. I heard the murmur of voices, felt the baby lifted out of my arms to be bathed or changed. A blessed languor kept me in a state of half-dreaming. If I didn't know better I'd have thought that Rea dosed me with something. Her worry about me was justified when I thought back to the exhaustion I'd felt during the last months of the pregnancy.

Harold came and went, his frustration at not being able to spend the night with his new family plain on his features--but there was barely enough room in the tent for my mother.

It was a full week before Finna announced she had to get back. "Your father is moving from Halston," she announced with a sly smile. "I never would have believed we could have a life together."

"I'm so glad for you, Mum. You need each other."

Alex and Finna had been apart since the day he basically kidnapped me and moved to the States. I was barely three at the time. The prophecy was the straw for my father. He was a practical man who couldn't believe in Otherworld or the prophecy. It took my trip here and my disappearance to bring him to his senses.

When Finna kissed me and said goodbye I was not sorry to see her go. I was ready to be with my mate and my baby and celebrate our new addition privately. Harold had already prepared a small shelter made of logs and limbs and covered over with canvas. I joined him on the afternoon of my mother's departure.

While I took care of Airmid, Harold set traps for the rabbits that had become so plentiful in the past months, skinning them before covering them with wild herbs and setting them over the fire. With the baby taking so much energy I was ravenous, and happy not to be the one doing the cooking. When the baby was sleeping Harold and I made plans and talked about our future. We'd been living here and there since the war; it was time we had a place of our own. Despite the nagging low-level anxiety that refused to go away, I was looking forward to my own garden, my own house, and settling into a normal life.

Chapter Two

harold slipped from under the dark canopy, his gaze going to where Maeve sat with her back against a tree feeding their baby. She looked like a renaissance painting, bright red hair fanned out around her shoulders, eyes downcast, lashes dark against her skin. Her exposed breast was a pale orb, the baby's tiny hands clenching and unclenching as she fed. He pulled the two plump rabbits from his belt and made sure he approached in her line of sight. For some reason she'd become jumpy and nervous and he didn't want to cause her another fright. It always left her breathless and disturbed, as though she expected some monster to suddenly appear. He chalked it up to hormones.

She looked more rested, although there was still a dark smudge beneath her eyes. If they were at home in the States the baby would be on a schedule and her rest would be less disturbed. Here in Otherworld it was as if any discipline she'd ever had was gone in favor of on demand feeding and no sleeping routine whatsoever. After nearly two months he had hoped to be intimate, but it was obvious Maeve was not ready, the baby waking her in the middle of the night more times than he could count. He let out a long sigh as he crouched next to her. "If you can put a pot of water on to boil I'll blanch them and skin them."

She looked up, her eyes unfocused. "Oh—yes, of course. But not until Airy has finished." She gave him a wan smile.

"I wish she was on a schedule," he muttered, heading to the creek with the pot.

He was anxious to be out of here, itching to begin work on their house. He'd been planning it for months, plans that he'd kept to himself, hoping to surprise her with his designs when the time came. Maeve had told him in no uncertain terms that she wouldn't leave until she could walk a mile without getting winded, her other stipulation that the baby be settled into a routine. But how could the baby settle into a routine if Maeve continued with on demand feeding? As it was the baby slept between them, making it impossible for him to even roll over and take Maeve in his arms.

When he came back with the water she'd fallen asleep, the baby asleep at her breast. He gently removed Airmid and swaddled her, placing her on the soft moss before getting to work on heating water. It would be a while before dinner was ready, he thought, feeling slightly miffed. But then he felt bad about his unkindness—Maeve was doing the best she could. It was a miracle things had gone as well as they did after the stress during the first trimester.

Airy was perfect in every way and his heart filled with love every time he looked at her. It was only his selfishness that made him want to rush things. Maybe it was the warrior role he no longer had, the new one he needed to develop—that of husband and provider. Husband. What a concept. He smiled to himself, imagining going down on one knee to propose. Maeve would laugh if he did something so romantic, and yet he had come to realize that he had a romantic soul. Why else would he still be harboring the Kenneth part of him and missing the war?

"I'm sorry," he heard her say, pulling him from his reverie. "I'm still so tired all the time."

"What would you like with the rabbit?" he asked, dipping them into the boiling water before laying them on another patch of moss. It would be easy to remove the fur now and drive a sharpened stick through the carcass for roasting over the fire.

"How about some rice pilaf, or spinach and cheese ravioli—tomato aspic, maybe?"

Harold chuckled. "If you'd asked for asparagus I could have found some a month or so ago. It grows wild in the marshy areas. And potatoes are plentiful now that they've been introduced. Unfortunately we don't have a garden or a root cellar. I've planned one for our house, by the way. Your choices today are cattail roots or watercress."

She rolled away from the tree and pushed herself up to standing, stretching her arms over her head. "Anything, Harold. I'm not really very hungry."

Harold frowned. "You have to keep up your strength, Maeve. I want to leave for Tiadan soon. If you don't eat properly you'll never make it for that mile walk you've been talking about."

"You've become such a nursemaid since Airy was born. I don't remember you ever nagging me about my diet before."

"And I've never been this fucking bored. If I don't start building our house soon I may lose it."

Maeve opened her mouth in surprise. "I didn't know. I'm sorry for holding you up." She put her arms around his neck.

Before he could stop himself he'd pulled her close. "God, Maeve, I'm dying here. I need—"

She pulled away and waggled a finger at him. "What you need is to give me time, Harold. I just had a baby and I'm not properly healed yet. Don't you think I--?"

At that point Airy woke up, her howls bringing Maeve instantly to the baby's side.

"I swear she has an uncanny way of knowing whenever we're having an intimate moment," he complained, turning back to the rabbit preparation.

"She does not," Maeve scoffed, unwrapping her from the tightly swaddled fabric. "She only needs changing."

Harold watched her cooing to the baby, the deft way she took care of the diaper. She was a good mother. An unmistakable feeling of jealousy moved through him as he watched her. Those same hands could be tending to him. He shook the feeling away and went to the stream to find some watercress.

Everything would happen in its own time.

CHAPTER THREE

It was a little over two months before we decided the baby was old enough and I was sufficiently strong to put our plan into motion. I'd finally managed to walk a mile, or at least I thought it was around a mile, without becoming so exhausted I needed a nap afterwards. Harold had been chomping at the bit for a while and I hated to see him so agitated, but he also tried very hard to be patient.

With Rea's help we made a papoose out of willow twigs and muslin so Airmid could ride on my back. We saddled Pooka, my creature of magic who took the shape of a black horse, and Argyll, Harold's enormous piebald, and rode west toward Tiadan. The village was one of only a few that had been spared the fires, looting and killing visited on most of Otherworld during the war. It sat on a high promontory with a view of the sea, the ocean breezes keeping it temperate all year round. Harold had made the trip once on his own already, coming back to report that he'd found the perfect spot for our house.

It was fall now and the day we chose to leave was crisp, the sky so blue it almost hurt to look at it. Leaves had turned varying shades of red and orange and yellow, and the mossy understory was pungent, pleasant scents of rotting leaves assailing our senses as the horses kicked up the loamy earth. In the Gregorian calendar it was late October, but in the ways of the people who lived here it was nearing Samhain, the beginning of the dark time. The celebration of the last harvest was upon us, and with it the cycle of life came full circle, bringing to mind all the spirits who had passed. For Harold and myself and many others, it was bittersweet, a time to remember all those who had given their lives to save Otherworld. Brandubh was gone, his minions with him. Gertrude, my psychic friend from Milltown, had disappeared at the end of the last battle and hadn't been seen since. I tried to turn my thoughts away from those last terrible days. The last festival of the Celtic year was to be held at the dolmen and would be a time of rejoicing.

I'd hoped that my sense of unease would go away now that we were about to begin our new life, but the anxiety remained. Several times I'd begun to tell Harold and then stopped myself. It would only worry him. My best bet was to go to the festival alone and talk with MacCuill. At least the druid wouldn't head off in warrior mode to do battle with an unseen enemy, as I knew the Harold/Kenneth duo would. But it would take a bit of manipulation to convince him to stay behind.

I pushed Pooka up beside Argyll. "What would you think about staying in Tiadan and working while I go to the festival? The sooner you start the sooner we can move in."

Harold looked over at me, his eyes mossy in the gloom of the Yew forest. "I'll do whatever you want, my love."

I made a derisive sound in the back of my throat. "Since when are you so accommodating?"

Harold grinned and pointed toward where the baby slept against my back. "Since that one joined us I'm pretty much willing to do anything."

"I thought you might want to get the house done before winter."

Harold's gaze went into the distance, a closed expression coming onto his features. "I guess you're worried about living with Tannith. She's a really nice person, Maeve."

"I don't know her, but I'm sure it will be fine," I assured him. "You like her and that's good enough for me."

"She keeps goats and makes cheese," he continued. "She'll probably be busy most days." He glanced over at me. "There won't be much privacy."

"Another reason you might want to get the house done sooner rather than later."

I watched his brows pull together in thought. When he finally grinned I let out my held breath.

"As long as you aren't meeting some long lost love."

"What in the world prompted that comment?" I asked. "You are my only love, Harold. You know that." I reached across and squeezed his upper arm, realizing how much I missed our intimacy. "Maybe by the time I get back, we—"

He swiveled in the saddle. "If your next words have to do with our physical relationship I'll be more than happy to stay here and work."

Tannith's house stood close to the Yew forest at the edge of a steep cliff overlooking the sea. A small herd of goats grazed on the grassy verge along a hillside that stepped downward in natural ledges. "This is a beautiful spot," I said, gazing at the dark water that stretched into the distance.

"There you are!" a voice called. I turned to see a stout woman in her fifties with gray streaks in her otherwise black hair. She had a kind face and an open smile. She came forward to help me off Pooka. "I knew you'd be here today."

Harold laughed. "I sent word with Dougal when we left Caer Sidi. It isn't hard to calculate how long it would take us."

Tannith let go of my arm and turned. "Are you saying my psychic powers are lacking?"

Harold grinned. "Not at all. Where is Dougal, by the way?"

"He's with his wife who is very pregnant, just like nearly every other woman in the village. My skills as midwife will be put to the test once all these babies start to arrive." She took hold of Airy's papoose and loosened the contraption from my back. "I'm so glad you've decided to build here," she continued, her brown eyes gazing at me warmly.

My attention was taken to the forest of green that filled in the space between the cliff and the valley, the robin's egg blue sky against the dark green. "I hope where we build is as beautiful as this."

Tannith smiled, her attention on the baby who was now pulling at a strand of her hair. "Did you know Tiadan has the best bow makers in all of Otherworld? They're fashioned from the sacred Yew trees that grow here."

"Where should I take the horses?" Harold interrupted.

"I have a small barn just there," she said, pointing down the hill toward a rustic wooden building hidden amongst the trees. "I keep the goats inside when the weather is bad and there's a place to store the tack."

I watched Harold lead the horses away before following Tannith toward the house. "My grandfather made me a bow when I first arrived in Otherworld."

"Ah yes, the infamous Eron. How is he?"

"I haven't seen him in months. I think he's traveling outside Otherworld."

"Really? I never would have thought he'd leave this place." She stared into the distance with a wistful expression. "He is a most attractive man."

She was attracted to my grandfather? "Yes, I guess he is," I responded, trying to think of him in this way and failing miserably.

"Come on in," she said, pulling open the door. "It's time I take you inside for a cup of tea."

Tea was made to the accompaniment of Tannith chattering about everything, from where she got her eggs—farmer just down the road--to the weather and how fine it had been, the new inn for travelers that was being built on the other end of town, and all the local gossip. By the time I thought of something to add she'd be on to another subject, her hands busy molding cheese into rounds and covering them in muslin. When the baby fussed in my lap I opened my dress, my head lolling back against the chair while I drowsed to the sound of Tannith's voice.

When Harold walked through the doorway twenty minutes later I opened my eyes, meeting his gaze. He took one look at me and went over to Tannith. "I think my lady needs a rest," he said, placing his hand on the older woman's shoulder. "Where will we be sleeping?"

She started and then laughed. "It's so nice to have company for a change," she said, wiping her hands on her apron. "I guess I've been carrying on more than I should." She smiled at me apologetically before leading the way up a narrow wooden stairway.

Once we were in the small loft bedroom with the door firmly closed I took hold of Harold's hand. "You can't build fast enough for me," I whispered.

Harold gathered me close, his breath warm in my ear. "I've decided to take your suggestion. That way we'll be in our house before Yule."

I giggled. "Yule?"

Harold broke up laughing. "When in Rome and all that...."

Three days later I was packed and ready to go. Harold saddled Pooka and strapped the canvas bag full of supplies on behind the saddle before giving me a leg up. "There's enough food in there to last you a week," he said, patting the heavy bag. He tightened Airy's papoose before moving to the front of Pooka where he took hold of the reins. "I guess I can't ask you to call me, can I?"

I laughed, trying to arrange my long dress so that it covered more of my legs. My deerskin boots given to me by my grandfather only came up mid-calf. "I don't often miss the electronics of our age, but it would be nice to check in when we're apart."

Harold placed his hand on my arm, his gaze going to the sleeping baby on my back. "I hate to be apart right now, but I

26

know you're right about this Good that things have settled down in Otherworld, otherwise I'd never let you go off on your own."

"And if I weren't sure, I wouldn't take our baby on a two-day trek all by myself." I laughed. "Remember who I am, Harold. As long as the baby hasn't sapped my powers I'm still the Willow. Do you still have that map?"

Harold pulled the worn parchment out of his pocket. "Almost forgot to give it to you." He opened it and pointed to some scribbling that immediately began to appear. "Considering how this map works I would say follow this trail," he said, running his finger along a line that zigzagged across the paper, "and then cross the river here and continue up toward the hill with the dolmen on top."

I watched the lines connect and move along the side where a mountain range had been penciled in before I grabbed it out of his hands. I was irritated that he felt the need to explain a magic map that was purely meant for me. I folded it and placed it in the pocket of my wool cloak.

"Give us a kiss," Harold said, pulling on my arm.

"Your speech patterns are changing," I said, bending down to place my lips on his.

When we pulled apart he looked up at me frowning. "I may have picked it up from the people here—does it bother you?"

I smiled and shook my head. "Just an observation, my king."

Harold grinned. "Be safe, milady, and when you get back your king will make you very welcome." He waggled his eyebrows suggestively.

I laughed. "I think I know what that means." I waved and kicked Pooka into a trot and headed down the well-worn trail, but once I was out of sight my eyes welled with tears. In all our time together I'd never hidden my feelings from him. If something bad happened to Airmid on this trip I would never forgive myself.

The map's route followed the edge of a narrow canyon, the trail narrowing and growing steep the further I went. As we gained elevation Pooka's hooves dislodged rocks and pebbles, the sound echoing away as they bounced and skittered into the abyss that loomed on our right. When Airmid began a mewling cry I found myself relieved to stop. I moved away from the canyon edge to dismount.

While I fed Airy my thoughts flew into the past to the last time I'd ridden by here. The memory was not a good one. My followers and I had been chased down into this very canyon trying to escape Brandubh's troops. But when we reached the valley floor what we found was even more horrifying than the fear of being caught. Hundreds of ravens were feeding on the dead and dying left behind by the enemy, the bodies contorted and bloody in the mud. When I approached, the ravens had lifted angrily from their feast, the cawing a grating sound that I could still hear.

When I shook my head to clear my thoughts it dislodged the baby who let out a whimpering cry. Once she was settled again I gazed upward toward the branches of oaks and beech trees, surprised to see that many of their leaves had already fallen. Most of the forests I'd been in recently were evergreen and I hadn't noticed the approach of winter. I didn't look forward to snow and ice, the memory of the former frozen wasteland of Otherworld too close for comfort. The arrival of the sun after those dismal months had been one of the happiest moments of my life.

When I heard the wind rustle through the few leaves that clung to the branches, the dry sound brought more disturbing memories. But the sky I could see in between the branches was cerulean blue with puffy white clouds moving by. The air smelled fresh and I could hear the buzz of bees in the late blooming flowers next to the trail. Everything was fine; there was nothing to worry about.

It was only a minute later that an enormous raven appeared at the lip of the canyon, startling me so much that I dropped the apple I'd bitten into. The apple rolled away and disappeared over the cliff edge. The raven watched me, its dark eye intelligent and knowing. *The war is over*, I told myself, holding the baby close. *The ravens are my friends now. They are no longer bewitched.* But the bird didn't move from its spot, its beady eye fastened on me. "What do you want?" I finally asked, a frisson of fear snaking up my spine. The bird lifted off on wings as black as night and flew away.

I let out my held breath and tried to slow my heartbeat. I wondered if the bird was a scout sent to report on my whereabouts—that's what Brandubh had used them for. I let out a sound between a laugh and a moan, realizing that I didn't know what the bird was about, only that my normal ability to discern patterns and intents had fled, leaving me vulnerable and afraid. Anxiety was not my friend.

I picked up the papoose, but when I tried to put Airmid back inside it, the baby let out such a wail I had to stop. "What's wrong, Airy?" She continued to cry as I examined the papoose for stinging bugs and unwrapped her covering to make sure nothing had stung her. I changed the piece of doubled over woven cloth that acted as a diaper and placed the dirty one in another muslin bag to wash later. But the baby would not be consoled. Eventually I had to leave her, red-faced and crying, on a patch of moss in order to retie the canvas bag of food on the back of the saddle.

I had nearly finished when the crying abruptly stopped. I heard the sharp caw of a raven and turned to see Airy poised at the very edge of the cliff. "Airy, no!" I sprinted the few feet to grab her just before she slipped over. The raven was in the sky now, dark wings glistening in the sunlight as the bird soared over the rocky chasm that loomed below. Others joined with him, their movements perfectly coordinated in a dance that seemed like a harbinger of death.

I rocked the baby for a long time before my own heart began to come into a normal rhythm again. This time Airmid was asleep when I deposited her into the papoose and strapped it firmly on my back. I re-mounted the black and headed up the trail, glad when the deer path widened and turned away from the cliff. As soon as the ground leveled out I pushed Pooka into a gallop, attempting to leave my morbid thoughts behind as we raced helter skelter across the uneven ground.

Chapter Four

Harold watched until Maeve was out of sight, a prickly sensation moving up both his arms. He rubbed them, but it seemed more like a premonition than a physical reaction to anything. Something seemed off with her but he couldn't put his finger on it. She wasn't devious by nature and he knew her well enough to realize she was hiding something. And her immediate and loud denial when he joked about her meeting someone was another indicator. They'd been together nearly every minute since the war ended and he doubted seriously that she had formed a relationship of that nature while pregnant with his baby. No. She must be worried about something and hadn't bothered to share. But if that was the case why did she take off alone with their baby?

"What's wrong, Harold?"

He turned to see Tannith standing in the doorway. "Nothing. It's just—"

"It's just that your lady love has taken off on her own and you're worried about her?"

He nodded. "We haven't been apart since the end of the war, and I tend to worry more now that we have a baby."

Tannith laughed. "Otherworld is safe now because of you and Maeve. Enjoy your time away from the crying child and put your mind to buildin' that house of yours."

"Crying child? Airy hardly ever cries."

"Just a figure of speech, Harold." She took hold of his shoulders and turned him to face away. "Now go to work before I have to get heavy-handed."

Harold let her give him a little shove. "I'll see you in a few hours," he grinned, heading away.

"Come back for dinner. I'm making Shepherd's pie."

Food was the last thing on his mind but he had to admit that lamb and mashed potatoes made his mouth water. Tannith was one of only a few people who had a large garden and had planted some of the vegetables he was used to. Potatoes, beans, eggplant and pepper plants were fallow now, but the potatoes would stay fresh in the ground and could be dug until the freeze came.

Maeve's grandfather, Eron, was responsible for what Tannith grew, bringing seeds on his former visits. After the loss of Catriona the man had needed solace, and Tannith was very good at that. But Harold knew that Tannith was half in love with Eron and had hoped for something more. Unfortunately Eron still grieved and probably would for many years to come. It was sad to think of a life given to eternal grieving when a good woman would be happy to love him; life was meant to be lived.

⌒⌇⌒

"Where have you been, man?" Dougal called out. Harold looked up to see his friends hard at work, the sound of hammering piercing his consciousness for the first time.

"Had to see Maeve off," he answered, climbing the last little rise. He looked over the framework of the house he'd designed without benefit of computer, or even a pencil and piece of paper. It had come from his head and he'd worked on it for months before he began to build. Maeve had left for the festival before he had a chance to show it to her.

Who could have predicted that his accounting job a year ago would be left behind to follow Maeve into an alien world? Or that he would have a new baby and build a house on a bluff overlooking an ocean that seemed to go on forever? He shook his head, a grin coming across his face.

"If ye stop moonin' over yer lady ye might have somethin' to show her when she returns," Iain called, the big man grinning at him from where he perched on top of the framework.

The rest of the day was spent framing and getting ready for the next phase. If they kept up this pace it would only be a month before the roof was on and they could move in. It would be rustic living until he built the cabinets and their bed, and put all the finishing touches on everything, but at least they'd be in their own house.

It was nearly time to quit when he had the vision—he dropped the hammer, hearing it clatter as it spun to the ground. Something wasn't right.

"What is it?" Iain called. "Ye see a spirit?"

Harold stared at his friend, unable to form words. Finally he said, "Maeve may be in trouble."

Iain laughed. "From bein' with you, I'd imagine."

"I'm serious, Iain. I saw her in the forest and there was a look on her face I haven't seen since the war."

"Since when do you have visions?" Dougal called from where he hung on the framework, hammering split logs into place.

Harold shrugged, trying to shake off the feeling of doom. "The baby's with her," he muttered.

"Isn't Maeve the Willow?" Dougal continued. "I'd imagine she could take care of herself without her brawny man along, who is a worrywart, if ye ask me."

"I didn't ask you," Harold said, trying to make light of what he'd seen. "But you're probably right. I'm sure she's fine. But I'll be very relieved when she returns."

"Relieved, is that what ye call it?" Iain joked.

"She just had a baby," Harold grumbled, not wanting to discuss his sex life.

"Hasn't it been two months already?" Iain said. "That's plenty of time—my lady was ready for me a lot earlier than that. Maybe she's been savin' herself for another, Harold—maybe she's meetin' someone at the festival."

Harold knew the man was joking but it was too close to what he'd been worrying about. "If it's all the same to you I say we quit now and take this up early tomorrow," he said, climbing down and putting his tools away.

"Don't take anything Iain says seriously," Dougal said quietly as he went by. "See you bright and early if it doesn't rain."

Harold looked up at the sky that was taking on a purplish tone as the sun disappeared. There wasn't a cloud in it.

Chapter Five

When a wooded area appeared on the map I headed there to spend the night. Oddly it was not familiar to me; I was sure I'd been in these woods many times in the past. I shook away my nerves and untacked Pooka, turning him loose to forage while I set up camp. Before I went to search for wood I placed the baby on a soft blanket of pine needles, keeping a wary eye out as I headed under the trees. I was nervous as a cat. And the further away from Harold I got the more nervous I became. Why had I been so intent to make this trip by myself?

As far as I could tell this was not part of the enchanted forest, and yet I heard voices in the distance calling my name and felt as though I was being watched. The baby seemed to feel the same unease, her restless mewling becoming more pronounced as the hours went by. I scanned into the shadows, trying to decide where the voices were coming from, but one minute they seemed to emanate from my left, the next minute from my right.

I had no idea how late it was when I finally wrapped my arms around the baby and pulled a cloak over us. But my unease would not go away, and my sleep was shallow and filled with dreams.

"I am not surprised to see you here," Cerridwen said. "You drank from the cauldron of knowledge and wisdom, you have given birth to the child who will also play a part in the unfolding drama of life. What is it you ask of me?"

I stared at the crone who had formerly appeared to me as a beautiful young woman. This goddess was far from beautiful; her parchment cheeks were sunken, her skin withered and dry. She was bent over, a dowager's hump along her upper back. "I'm only dreaming," I replied, looking down at the baby in my arms.

"You may think this is a dream, but it is not. You are here because you feel the encroachment of something you cannot explain. It is in its infancy, just as the child you hold in your arms, but if it is not brought into the light it will surely grow. You have a question but it is not yet formed in your mind. I will see you again when you know what to ask. Until then, take care of your child."

I woke with a start, unable to see anything. For a moment I forgot where I was, a scream moving up my throat, but then I heard Pooka nicker and remembered. Aside from that comforting sound there was only the rustling of night animals foraging for food. But now that I was wide-awake there would be no more chance of sleep. My sleeping baby hardly registered the movement of being picked up and carefully slipped into her papoose.

CER

I rode through the rest of the night, my fears growing as Pooka trotted along the only trail available. It was narrow with a drop-off on one side that was barely visible in the dark. Consulting the map proved impossible, my only hope that the horse wouldn't stumble and go over the edge. When we finally arrived at a wider track the sky had turned pale mauve, streaks of peach, pink and gray heralding the sunrise in the east. I pulled on the reins and brought Pooka to a stop and retrieved the map, my worry receding as lines appeared. The dolmen wasn't far.

By the time we reached the sacred hill and the megalithic tomb came into view I let out an exhausted sigh. The entire trip had been made worse by Airy's crying, and nothing I did made any difference. I wondered if it was the atmosphere that had set her off; she was my baby and certainly sensitive to energies. Too bad my sensitivity seemed to be lacking at the moment. Aside from nerves I had little understanding of what was bothering me. In the past I'd had clues and visions to help me along. This was new and I didn't like it.

When I rode up the last hill and descended into the valley there were hundreds of people setting up camp. The chatter of conversation came to my ears, loud shouts when someone dropped their load of wood, laughter as friends re-united. Men carried armloads of wood to the top of the hill for the bonfire, placing them down and heading away for more.

The last time I was here the woods were nearly dead from lack of water and cold. Now the conifers were lush, the sparse areas filled in with young trees. It did my heart good to see it. That and the joyful festive atmosphere raised my spirits. I waved to MacCuill who was standing with a group of druids. I was glad to be here among friends.

I was dismounting when MacCuill hurried toward me. "I didn't expect you this early. Where is Harold?" He helped me off, his gaze going to the foam covering Pooka's neck. "And what did you do to this horse?" Before I could answer another druid arrived, bowing to me before leading Pooka away.

"I'm being treated like royalty," I remarked, watching him pull off the tack and begin to walk my horse to cool him down.

MacCuill lifted Airy from her papoose. "You *are* royalty, Maeve." He stared at me quizzically. "Your horse is covered in sweat and you seem on edge—did you and Harold have a quarrel?"

"No. He's working on our house and trying to get it completed so we can move in. Pooka is sweaty because I rode all night. Better that than be overtaken by some malevolent force."

His eyes narrowed. "What are you talking about?"

But the baby let out a wail before I could answer him and I had to take her out of the druid's arms to calm her down. "I think she must be hungry," I told him before settling against a tree trunk to feed her.

MacCuill frowned, watching me. "We can talk later," he finally said, turning to head back up the hill.

Once Airy was fed and calm again I looked around for MacCuill, hoping to resume our conversation. But now his attention was on the preparations for the bonfire. More villagers, Wildmen, Crion and druids were arriving, their carts full of foodstuffs to share from the last harvest. I watched them unpacking their goods, reuniting with friends as they organized the vegetables and fruits, the eggs and chicken carcasses and cheeses. There would be a feast.

I was in the middle of admiring Rea's newborn baby boy when MacCuill sought me out, his face creased with concern.

"So what is this about a malevolent force?" he asked once we reached a secluded spot away from the others.

I gazed around at the smiling faces, hearing laughter ring out and echo across the hillside. The day was clear and warm, a soft breeze touching my cheek like thistledown. Pale mauve grasses swayed in the breeze, the last sunflowers turning their faces to the bright orb that hung in the sky. It was hard to even remember what I'd experienced at the cliff edge or the feelings that had driven me to saddle up in the middle of the night and ride hard through the forest. "I don't know what it is. Something seemed off on the way here. I've been feeling like this for a while—like something is replaying."

"Brandubh is dead, Maeve. You saw him disappear under water and get caught up in the currents. And the Oillteil who bowed down to him are gone. What could possibly be replaying?"

Nerves clenched in my stomach as I recalled what happened at the cliff edge. "The baby nearly rolled into the canyon, MacCuill. I reached her just in time. I've never been so frightened in my life, even during the worst of the war. And not only that," I continued, noticing his skeptical expression. "A huge raven landed on the edge and sat there staring at me. It reminded me of Brandubh."

"The ravens are no longer bewitched and seem perfectly fine to me. I think motherhood has affected your perceptions." He smiled, patting me on the shoulder. "Who is to say the raven wasn't there to protect you, Maeve?"

I shook his hand away, annoyed that he was making light of this. "I know what I saw. You haven't felt it or heard any rumors?"

MacCuill stared at me without expression. "Queen Druantia has not mentioned a change, nor have the goddesses. Your hormones must be out of balance."

I thought about that for a moment—he could be right. I'd heard stranger things about women's emotions after they gave birth. And having a new baby was making me much more alert to danger. But..."It started before Airy was born. I didn't have raging hormones then."

He shrugged dismissively. "I don't know what to say. I would think if something were going on I would be aware of it." When another druid shouted his name he turned. "I have to help with the bonfire. We'll talk later." I watched him walk slowly up the hill, struck for the first time that he was getting older.

"Is your wee mother coming for the celebration?" Duncan asked, arriving behind me.

Despite his reluctance to engage in such practices I turned to hug my old friend. Duncan had been my self-appointed guardian during the war, his sense of humor and watchfulness a blessing to me as well as my disparate group of followers. "I haven't seen her since Airy was born. I suppose she's busy with my father. Last I heard he was moving in with her."

Duncan laughed. "Aye. A rekindled love."

I didn't respond, my attention taken by a group of strangers who had appeared at the crest of the hill. I pointed. "Who are they?"

Duncan turned and squinted, shading his eyes. "I dinna recognize them. Maybe they came from the western forest—part of Dagda's men?"

I shook my head. They were slight in build with dark skin and hair, their clothing either black or dark brown. Dagda's soldiers were broad shouldered with reddish-gold hair, and they wore leather. "I don't think so."

Duncan shrugged. "Part of the Fae then?"

When Duncan wandered away to help with wood carrying, I settled under a tree to feed Airy again. The baby seemed unusually restless. I kept a close eye on the newcomers, not surprised when they received uncomprehending stares from the groups already assembled. They didn't mingle as they scanned across the hillside. They seemed furtive, like criminals who were checking out their victims. They reminded me of the dark birds at the canyon. Could a flock of birds take on human shape? I shivered at the thought. Who were they?

Chapter Six

Night fell quickly, the day taken like a wounded
soldier as flaming colors of blood splashed across
the western sky. I watched the dark encroach, my fears growing
as the minutes went by. Somehow the strangers had taken away
my earlier calm. Now when I scanned for them I couldn't see if
they were here or not. It made me nervous, as though they
might appear behind me when I least expected it. Was this a
premonition or just my wild hormones as MacCuill had
suggested? I was glad to be in a crowd of people I mostly
knew.

"Maeve."

When I looked up I expected to see one of the dark men,
but instead a druid was standing there. "Yes, I'm Maeve. Who
are you?"

Deep gray eyes peered at me from under shaggy brows.
"I'm Gunner. In the future I will come to know your daughter,
Airy."

His tone was somber, dour even. I wondered what exactly he knew about my daughter's future. I glanced inside my hastily erected hovel of sticks and boughs to make sure the baby hadn't time traveled away. "You speak of the future as though it's already here."

"Maybe it all happens simultaneously. Have you thought of that?"

"I've read theories about such a thing, but haven't really thought too deeply about it. I've always felt that the future was something fluid and flexible." I laughed nervously. "I wouldn't want to know what was going to happen."

"Then I won't tell you," he responded.

I wanted to ask him why he was here, but something held me back. There was a seriousness about him that bordered on severity. "Are you part of the dark-haired group?" I asked, pointing to the vicinity of where I'd last seen the newcomers. Of course it was pitch black now with no sign of anyone except the low campfires that burned here and there, laughter splitting the silence every so often.

"I am not sure which group you speak of, but I assure you that aside from being a druid I am not part of any faction, category, association, union or fraternity. MacCuill and I have known one another for a long time now. I'm here to talk with you because he mentioned your trepidation regarding the change in energies."

'Long time' had to mean a century or so. MacCuill had taken me seriously—seriously enough to mention my worries to this man, who seemed the epitome of competence. He waited for me to answer with a look on his face that I found intimidating. He was not at all like MacCuill, who had a bear-like quality to him as well as a smile that could light up a small city. This man was tall, bordering on gangly, wearing clothes of greens and browns that reminded me of camouflage. Could I confide in him?

"In the past months I've noticed a change," I began hesitantly. "I can't really explain what, only that something feels different. And the group I mentioned who arrived earlier seemed out of place. They made me nervous."

"Is it the men or the energies you're most concerned with?"

"Are you an investigator?" I laughed, trying to get him to smile, but his expression didn't change.

"I suppose a druid might fall into that category from time to time, but that is not my function here."

I waited for him to elaborate and when he didn't, I said, "The men seemed to bring on more of the unease I've been feeling. So I guess both would be true." At that moment the baby woke and I crawled inside the shelter. When I looked out again the druid was gone. I carried Airy outside, scanning for Gunnar in the dark, but he'd melted into the shadows.

I woke in the morning after a disturbing dream in which Brandubh and the Oillteil were roaming across the countryside. They had already set fire to the eastern conifer forests where Cernunnos ruled, and were moving on to the hardwood forests on the western side of Otherworld. The war was beginning all over again. I felt faint with fear when I remembered the very real death and destruction, and the part I played in releasing Otherworld from his grip. The thought of it happening all over again was horrifying. Before I was able to make sense of the imagery Airy woke, her high-pitched cries taking all of my attention. Waking in distress was not normal for Airy and the recent change worried me.

I was carrying a load of wood up to the top of the hill when MacCuill strode toward me. "Did you meet Gunner?"

"I did. He's a taciturn one, isn't he? He left before we got a chance to go into much detail."

MacCuill chuckled. "I have to admit he has little in the way of a sense of humor. He's a time traveler and as such I thought he might be able to help you."

"I figured that since he said he would know Airy when she was older. I guess that means he's already met her? I find that disturbing."

"Gunnar has a unique perspective on things since he is aware of the past and the future. And by the way, the men you mentioned were gone this morning."

"Who were they?"

"No one seems to know. My suspicion is that they came upon our camp and wondered what it was all about."

"So, no dark intent?"

MacCuill shrugged. "I didn't get any 'vibe', as you like to say. I did find their manner strange and also their sudden disappearance. I'm sorry about how I reacted to you yesterday, Maeve. I've been under considerable strain with this celebration. It's the first one in years that Queen Druantia has deigned to attend. You can understand that I want everything to go smoothly."

The druid queen was formidable with her flashing eyes and overbearing manner. "Yes. She can be scary when she's angered or put out. I don't envy you."

MacCuill didn't react to this, his gaze in the far distance. "We will have a full moon tonight." His dark eyes met mine. "This is a powerful time when departed spirits can join the living. There are many I expect to see once the moon is up."

I thought about all the Crion, Amuigh, Wildmen and Oillteil who had died in my name—followers who had deserted Brandubh to align themselves with me. The ape-like creatures of the Amuigh had been nearly driven to extinction during the years of Brandubh's rule. And the Tuatha de Danann leader, Dagda, had lost many of his warriors, both men and women. For me seeing any of the departed would bring all the pain back; it was hard enough saying goodbye the first time. "And Arianrhod?"

"The goddess of the moon will bless those who have departed and those who still live." He put his hand on my shoulder. "I expect you to join me in leading the celebration, Maeve. You will stand by my side and give the invocation."

"I don't know the words."

"I'll teach you. It isn't very long. Your followers and all the ones who came through unscathed need to hear the words from the lips of their savior."

"Savior—isn't that a bit over the top? Harold was part of it too, and what about all the other tribes and people who supported us?"

"Yes, but it was the 'Willow' who led them in the fight that wasn't a fight. Do not play down your role. You are revered here as the one who stopped what could have been the end of Otherworld." He took hold of my arm. "Come with me and we can go over what you need to say."

When it grew dark the soft breeze felt like velvet against my skin. There was something in the air that had softened the edges of everything. Flames danced and spit, turning blue and then gold. The night was full of magic.

"I'll take care of Airy," Rea told me, shooing me off to the top of the hill. I watched her cradle my baby, her newborn in a pack on her back.

By the time the moon showed its glorious orange-tinged face the enormous crowd had gathered by the dolmen, the chatter gone as they waited for the goddesses and gods to join us. In the distance I spied Cernunnos, wild hair curling around the antlers on his head. Another man stood next to him, a glow radiating all around him. "Who is that?" I whispered to MacCuill.

"That is Arawn, god of the underworld. Cerridwen must have brought him."

"I've never met him."

"He doesn't often show himself. He lives on an island in a place untouched by man; he only shows himself if he wishes to resurrect someone from the land of perpetual night. You do know by now that the underworld is not the Christian hell that it's touted to be?"

I nodded, watching Arawn and Cernunnos. "I've been there, MacCuill, but I did see several dead souls struggling to get back to the surface." I pulled my gaze away from the two magnificent gods. "I thought Cerridwen was the ruler there."

"There are always those who cannot accept their own deaths. They are the unconscious ones, the ones who believe that getting back to the land of the living is the most important thing there is. If they would but turn to face where they are they would see there is much richness there. And you are correct about Cerridwen. She is the crone goddess of the underworld, the keeper of the cauldron of wisdom and rebirth. But there are many gods and goddesses who reside in Anwnn."

"When I met her she appeared young and beautiful, but just lately I dreamed of her as crone."

"She is both crone and maiden. Did she have anything to say to you?"

"She acknowledged that something dark is encroaching."

MaCuill frowned, his expression concerned. "If she appears tonight we must have a talk with her," he said, glancing around at the hushed crowds who waited. He took my elbow. "It is nearly time to begin."

I had dressed in a green gown woven for me by the Crion, a braided belt around my waist. My hair had grown since the days when I cut it short, and now fell past my shoulders in loose curls.

"You look like a goddess," MacCuill whispered as he led me to the raised stone. "I will start and you chime in when I turn."

I nodded and took my place, hoping I could remember the hastily memorized words. A second later there was a cacophony of sound as everyone cheered. "To Willow!" they chanted. I bowed low and raised my hand to signal quiet and then MacCuill began.

"Tonight we come together to celebrate the New Year!" he called, his deep baritone ringing out. "We bring our blessings to those no longer with us as well as those who still walk this earth. The veil is thin tonight and if you wish you will see your friends and loved ones as they join us here." He glanced at me with a slight nod.

"This is a magical night when all that is unseen can be seen!" I continued in my best carrying voice. "Cerridwen, goddess of the underworld, will join us tonight as well as Arianrhod, the moon goddess who will bestow her blessings for the coming year! We rest now and wait for the fruition of the seeds we've planted, both literally and figuratively. Much new life has come into being and many more bairns will be born as the season turns from winter to spring. We..." I faltered and glanced at MacCuill.

"We gather to turn the wheel of the year," he continued smoothly, "to watch as the nights grow longer and the days grow shorter, knowing that the promise of spring and rebirth are ever in our hearts. And now we will feast and celebrate and wait for the arrival of the departed and our goddesses and gods who come to join us on this special night!"

A cheer went up as he finished, faces in the crowd flushed with happiness. I felt a tendril of fear. What if I were right? What if these people were no longer safe from harm? But MacCuill had taken my arm and was leading me off the stone and over to where the enormous pyramid of wood blazed and spit, bright sparks leaping into the darkness. A makeshift table had been set up, covered with every imaginable type of foodstuffs brought by the farmers from all over Otherworld. Pitchers of ale and mead were lined up behind the food, sure to be emptied quickly.

Everyone was dancing and singing when Arianrhod made her appearance, flying over the hill as an owl before landing next to the ancient stones and shifting into her human shape. "Maeve!" she said, reaching for my hands. "You look wonderful!" She glanced around. "Where is Airmid?"

I pointed behind me where Airy lay on the grass next to MacCuill and Gunner. I was just about to say something else when probably a hundred specters appeared in the air above the crowd. There were screams of recognition and then chaos as people rushed around, trying to get a chance to talk with the dead. I turned away, afraid to see if Gertrude or my grandmother were among them.

"Gertrude isn't there, and neither is Catriona," Eron said, appearing at my shoulder. My grandfather always knew what was on my mind. He drew me close, his familiar scent of sage and pine enveloping me. His life in woods or caves was that of a nomad, but he still was able to fashion his flutes and bows to sell and trade—beautiful works of art. A bag of them hung on his back, brought to trade or gift to friends. "I have not seen you since Airy was born." He picked up the baby, lifting her to get a good look at her. "She will resemble you," he said. "And her grandmother." His eyes darkened with sadness.

"I've missed you," I said, trying to distract him. "Where have you been all these months?"

"Traveling and trying to find Catriona."

I was sure my grandmother had perished during the war, but Eron refused to believe it. He was obsessed with finding her again, and I had the feeling his grief had played tricks with his mind. "Harold is building us a house in Tiadan," I told him, changing the subject.

He nodded. "I went by there on my way here. Harold misses you."

"I wish he were here, although…"

Eron waited, his eyes on mine. "Although, what?"

"I hesitate to talk about it here, tonight, but I've been feeling something— something—"

"Something off, wrong? I have also felt this. I hoped it was because of grief. Are you saying you have not spoken to Harold about this?"

I opened my mouth to continue when Airy let out a cry. "I think she needs you," Eron said, handing her over.

A moment later MacCuill put a hand on Eron's arm. "I need to talk to you." He led my grandfather away, and I watched them talking with their heads bent together. I wondered why MacCuill found it necessary to have a private conversation with Eron.

When I fed Airy I was barely able to keep my eyes open; it was very late and I was ready to go to sleep. But judging from the amount of ale and mead the revelers had consumed I figured the party would continue through the rest of the night.

I was drowsing when my gaze was drawn to the dolmen, surprised to see the black-haired men lurking along the back edge of the stones. The light from the fire clearly revealed their dark clad forms. One man walked a distance down the hill, apparently to get a better look at me. I was still feeding Airy, and at least a quarter mile away, and yet I felt the intensity of that stare. Something inside me stirred. Harold and I had not resumed relations since the baby was born and the sensation that moved through me was distinctly sexual. He held my gaze for several long moments and then turned away, signaling for his group to move on. He was obviously the leader, whoever they were. I watched them disappear over the lip of the hill, realizing that my heartbeat had quickened. It was a while before I was calm enough to think of sleep again. But when I finally drifted off I dreamed.

I was in a deep cave with a man who was not Harold. His skin was dark from the sun, laugh lines bracketing golden-amber eyes, dark hair in tangles around his angular face. When he took my hand I let him lead me to a bower of soft moss where he pushed me gently down. When he made love to me I responded, reveling in the exquisite sensations coursing though my body as we moved together. 'Who are you?' I whispered, but he didn't answer.

Chapter Seven

The silence when I woke in the morning was so profound it felt like all sound had been sucked from the air. There was not even a birdcall or the chirp of a cricket. Was this a consequence of what I'd been feeling? Surely the birds were up by now—had they all fled because of those dark bird-like men or was it simply that they were migrating due to the coming cold weather? I left Airy sleeping to go into the forest to relieve myself. When I got back she was beginning to stir, her eyes opening suddenly to gaze into mine. "Good morning, sweet one," I whispered, picking her up. I saw the hint of a smile on her face. When she let out a gurgle I decided that it was her first actual laugh. It was nice to have her wake calmly.

My gaze traveled across the hillside toward MacCuill's camp where I saw the druid making a fire, his movements slow. And where had Queen Druantia been the night before? I hadn't seen her—probably a blessing from what I knew of her demanding ways. I also had not had the chance to talk with Cerridwen, her arrival happening after I'd settled into my camp. I'd seen her talking with MacCuill and with others. Maybe the druid had mentioned my dream.

It was then that I remembered the dream I'd had the night before, my horrified gasp frightening the baby who pulled away and scrunched up her face. When she let out a wail I pressed her close. "It's okay, it's okay," I soothed, hoping her cries wouldn't wake the sleepers. In the meantime the feelings and visions from my dream assailed me. I felt guilt, as though I'd been unfaithful to Harold. It was just a dream, I assured myself. But I'd had other dreams that were something more, and this felt similar. I had no one to talk to about this other than Cerridwen, or possibly Rea. I could never admit to MacCuill what had happened in that intense encounter with the dark-haired stranger, especially since the druid always insisted that dreams were as real as waking life.

I had made a fire and was heating water for tea when MacCuill appeared, Gunnar by his side. "The night went well," MacCuill said, his savvy gaze trained on me as if he knew all about my dream. We had always had a telepathic link.

I turned away, a rush of heat coming into my cheeks. "Yes, I think it did. What time did everyone go to bed?"

MacCuill chortled. "It was nearing dawn." He glanced around at the sleeping camps, the few people up and tiredly making their fires. "It will be a slow day, I think."

"Is everyone leaving today?"

MacCuill nodded, turning to Gunnar. "We wanted to talk with you before you go, Maeve. Gunnar has told me something that I think you should know."

I glanced at the lean man with the unsmiling face. "About yesterday's group? I saw them again later."

Gunnar ran a hand through his straggly gray hair. "That group is led by Gan Ceanach. The ones with him are a band of Welsh fairies known as Bendith Y Mamou."

"I've never heard of him or them. What did they want here?"

"Did you sense anything?"

"No. Why?"

"Gan Ceanach is also known as 'love-talker'. He has been known to seduce women, causing them to become obsessed with him."

When his gray eyes bored into mine I laughed nervously. "That sounds a bit far-fetched. For what purpose?"

The druid shrugged. "There's not much reason for what he does other than conquest and the pleasure of the intimacy. No so with the others. What were they doing the second time you saw them?"

"One of them was staring at me, at least it seemed like he was. I could feel his power from a quarter mile away."

Gunnar glanced at MacCuill. "It is as we feared," he said.

"Feared? What does he want?"

MacCuill reached for the baby and rocked her for a moment before he answered. "He may be targeting you."

"Me? Why?"

"He needs an ally here. From what Gunnar has told me there's a fight brewing between two factions of faery."

"What can I do for him?"

"You are the most powerful person in Otherworld; if he approaches you, do not underestimate him."

I scoffed. "If he thinks I'm the most powerful person here, he's sadly misinformed. There are druids and gods and goddesses all over Otherworld. Is he evil?"

"I would not call him evil," Gunnar answered, "but I would call him devious. He was here for a reason."

I stared at the druid. "And you know what it is, don't you? You've already seen it."

Gunnar's gray eyes met mine. "What I have seen is not written in stone, Maeve. Many things can happen to change the future. Are you riding home alone?"

"Yes. I know the route and it's only a two day trip."

"I will accompany you," Gunnar said.

"I don't want to be accompanied. I can take care of myself."

When the baby began to wriggle MacCuill handed her back. "If Gan Ceanach wants something of you, you will not be able to deny him."

"MacCuill, do you think what I've been feeling is energy from the Fae?"

"Could be. There are many races of faery and they do not all get along. You need to tread carefully. I would feel better if you allowed Gunnar to ride with you to Tiadan."

I shook my head, the idea of the taciturn man's company for two days making me shudder. "I'll be fine. I have a fast horse and I have powers of my own."

Gunnar made a derisive sound. "Your powers are not close to what Gan Ceanach is capable of."

When I met his gaze I had a moment of fear. I had a baby now and a man who loved me. A shiver ran down both my arms—a premonition, and not a good one. I would not put my baby in jeopardy for any reason. I turned away to pour my tea before facing them again. "I'll be extremely careful and I'll take a shortcut. Does that meet with your approval?" I gazed from one to the other.

They exchanged a look. "We cannot force you," MacCuill answered. "If you do meet him or the rest of the group approaches you, you must keep your mind clear. If you don't they will take you over, and when they do, neither you nor your baby will be safe. If you need me I'll be at the castle."

"You're living at the queens's castle now? And by the way, why didn't she show?"

"A runner came to bring her regrets. She was feeling too unwell to make the trip. I'm there to help her until her time comes. It won't be long now."

MacCuill was very close to the queen and it shocked me to hear she was so near death. "Who will take over?"

"The druid counsel will decide."

I hugged them both goodbye, assuring them that I'd be on the lookout for Gan Ceanach and the Welsh fairies. "How do I handle this *love-talker* if I do come upon him?"

"There is no handling when it comes to Gan Ceanach. Just don't let him kiss you."

I scoffed. "Of course I won't let him—" But the sentence was left unfinished as another group of people came to say goodbye.

I had a bite to eat in between saying farewell to all the friends I'd seen. When Rea came by and I told her about Gan Ceanach her eyes went wide. "Most of the Fae left here before the war began. I didn't expect them back. Gan Ceanach is not to be trifled with, Maeve. Shall I come along for protection?"

"You?" I suppressed a giggle when I looked down on the slight woman who stood barely four feet tall. "I'll be fine, Rea."

"You do not know what he is capable of. A Crion woman was lost to us because of his charms."

"Lost? What does that mean?"

"She was obsessed with him, gave birth to a half Crion half faery baby." She stared at me with a worried look. "Gan Ceanach never returned and she died of love."

"Died of love? How is that possible?"

She shook her head, the other Crion women behind her acknowledging what she was saying with sage nods.

"Couldn't you get rid of the spell?"

"The only way to stop the spell is to find a witch strong enough to break it. At the time there was no one here who fit that description."

I wondered what I would do it that happened to me. "And now?" I asked.

"There are those who can help but it will not be easy to find them. Take great care, Willow, and keep that baby close. And bring Harold and come for a visit once your house is completed."

"Are you living in the tunnels?"

She smiled and nodded. "Our tunnels have been repaired now and there is laughter and the chatter of children for the first time in many moons. The sheep are back and we weave again. Yes, to the tunnels."

The first time I'd visited the tunnels and the diminutive Crion, I'd been astounded by their way of life, the beautiful tapestries that covered the earthen walls, the torches that burned in each room casting a warm glow across floors that looked baked with a glaze of burnt umber. It made me happy to know they were back where they belonged. I kissed the top of her tiny baby's fuzzy head and turned away to wipe at my tears. It would most likely be months before we saw each other again.

She hugged me as only Rea could and waved as she and her group turned to leave.

My uneasiness returned full force as I made haste to go. When I found Pooka near the stream with some other horses he turned his shimmering golden eyes to mine. The horse was one of my guardian spirits and had been since the first day I came upon him. Months and months ago, during the early days of the war, he'd offered himself as my mount and hadn't strayed since. It was Harold who recognized his true identity, telling me his name was Pooka for the shape shifting faery spirit he was. Pooka was Fae and would know if I were in danger. "Don't let me be bewitched by Gan Ceanach," I whispered as I placed the saddle on his back.

I mounted quickly and turned toward the trail, unable to take any more farewells. These were my friends and former followers, the people who had stood by me during the long months of war. I loved them all. What lay in the forest ahead of me was anyone's guess.

CHAPTER EIGHT

I had taken a different route through a hardwood forest when I heard a flute or a person singing. I brought Pooka to a stop to listen.

"Are you looking for me?"

I jumped in the saddle, nearly tumbling off the horse. When I looked down a man was standing by Pooka's head, his hand on the bridle. A mist lay around him, his golden eyes nearly the same color as Pooka's eyes. Shiny black hair hung straight to his shoulders. His intense stare gave me a shiver. "Are you Gan Ceanach?" I asked, fearing the worst.

He smiled and inclined his head. "At your service."

He held my gaze, and when I tried to speak I couldn't utter a word. Finally he grabbed my hand and helped me off the horse. He was shorter than I, his head barely reaching my chin, and yet he held a power that I couldn't deny. His features were even and perfect, his smile beguiling as only a faery's smile could be.

"You need a rest and the baby needs to eat," he said, pulling Airy out of her papoose and handing her to me.

I'd never been shy about feeding her in public, but for some reason I didn't want to bare my breasts in front of this man. "She's fine right now," I told him, reaching into my bag with one hand to grab a hunk of cheese. But of course as soon as those words were out of my mouth she began to howl, her face scrunching up as though someone was pinching her. I turned my back to him and fumbled around with my clothing. When she was settled I covered her with a blanket and lowered myself to the ground.

He sat next to me. "I hoped to catch up with you—did you see me at the dolmen? I have a proposition."

"What proposition? I've been told to stay away from you."

He laughed, his golden eyes twinkling in the dusky light of the forest. "I need you to align with me."

"Align myself for what?"

"To go against the ravens."

"The ravens." I thought of my experience at the canyon. "I thought something might be going on with them." When I turned, he caught my gaze with his own. I felt the sexual energy he exuded just as I had at the dolmen.

"Yes," he said, answering my unasked question. "I saw you there. I followed you."

"What's going on with the ravens?" I asked, noticing that they were perched in several of the trees.

"Morrighan has imbued the ravens with her evil intents and I have resolved to stop her—with your help of course." He smiled.

"But why would Morrighan do this? She was happy to be finished with the war and with Brandubh. At the end she cursed him."

He raised his eyebrows "You do know that Morrighan is the goddess of war? She has an agenda that I have not yet discovered; possibly she's bored."

When the baby's head lolled to one side he lifted her out of my arms and placed her gently on the moss. He leaned toward me and took my face in his hands. What had MacCuill warned--something about not letting him…but it was too late, his mouth was on mine and I melted against him as the kiss grew deeper. He tasted like summer rain. When one of his hands moved to my exposed breast, his touch sizzled against my skin, creating little waves of desire. I told myself to stop him, to say no, but I felt like a starving animal that had just been given food. When he removed my clothes I didn't feel the chill air, nor did the momentary thought of Harold remain in my mind. I was wholly Gan Ceanach's to do with as he pleased.

The next thing I knew I was lying naked on a bower of some soft material that hadn't been there before, his hands roaming across my body. At some point he'd removed his clothes and now I viewed his strong chest, the narrow hips. His body was compact compared to Harold's, narrower and more angular, but the part of him that I focused on was not in keeping with the rest of him. When I gasped he let out a delighted laugh.

As his fingers and lips played across my over-heated skin I drifted into a world I'd never been before, my body weightless and clinging to his as though he was the only thing keeping me from floating away. He was corporeal and at the same time ethereal, like an angel who had only lately discovered gravity. He was inventive and very thorough, and when it was over I lay panting, barely able to catch my breath. I gazed up at his handsome features, caught again by his golden eyes. "I thought I dreamed you."

He smiled, one finger tracing lightly along my collarbone. "You did dream me the other night, but having you here like this is a much better experience for both of us."

"I'm pledged to another. Harold and I have a baby."

His eyes flashed dark. "All that is superfluous—silly conventions that mean nothing in the real scheme of things. You will remain with Harold but your heart is mine now."

It was at that moment that I really felt his power, the iron-like hold he had over me. "But—" He ignored me as he rose and dressed quickly, and before I could utter another word he was gone, melting into the shadows without a sound. I called his name but he didn't answer.

My body needed more, as if the coupling had woken some sleeping beast inside me. I pulled on my dress in a daze. I felt sick with wanting him. When the baby woke I could barely pay attention to her. She wasn't important to me now, as if Gan Ceanach had taken all my love for himself. The crying finally penetrated to the part of me that was mother, but when I fed and changed her, my thoughts were far away. The feather touch of his fingers dancing across my skin came back to me, lighting my desire, an all-consuming flame. My heart yearned for him.

Chapter Nine

harold woke suddenly with his heart racing. He sat up in bed and tried to gather the wisps of the dream he'd had. Maeve was lost to him, her heart given to another. He ran his fingers through his tangled hair feeling like he might throw-up. Outside the pale gray of early dawn greeted his weary eyes. He had to work today, but what he wanted to do was ride like hell to find Maeve. She must be on her way home by now. The dream was only a dream, he told himself, but he couldn't stand the feelings running through his body. He felt desperate and afraid that she had pledged herself to another. He dressed and went downstairs, surprised to find Tannith already in the kitchen, a cup of tea on the table in front of her.

"You couldn't sleep either?" she asked, looking up.

"I had a nightmare," he said, sitting down next to her.

"Would ye like to talk about it?"

He shook his head but then began to talk despite himself. "Maeve was with another man—someone dark and small. He held a pipe and his eyes were a golden color I've never seen in a human being."

Tannith's eyes widened. "You just described a member of the Fae."

"Who?"

"An evil fairy by the name of Gan Ceannach. He is also called the 'love talker'."

Harold put his head in his hands. "Do you think this is more than a dream?"

Tannith gazed at him worriedly. "Let's hope not. If it is, Maeve is now under his spell and will be obsessed with finding him again. Ye will have to break the spell to get her back."

Harold stared at the older women, hoping she was teasing him, but her eyes were glazed with worry and the expression on her face was serious in the extreme. "Why would I dream it, Tannith? How could I know?"

"You and Maeve have been through a war together, Harold. You love her and she loves you. It isn't unheard of to have a psychic link like this. But for your sake I hope it was only a bad dream."

"Where do these Fae live?"

"They used to live here in Otherworld but they were driven out by the gods and goddesses. Fae are not all bad but they can be devious and mischievous and downright dangerous when they want something."

"But why would they be here now—and why Maeve?"

Tannith shrugged and took a sip of tea. "Your guess is as good as mine. He might want something from her, but what that is won't be revealed right away. Many times this faery leaves his victims to literally die from love."

"Does he—"

"Aye, Harold. It only takes one kiss, but usually it goes farther than that. He is like Don Juan in some ways—irresistible."

"Oh god," Harold moaned. "What do I do?"

"Ye wait until she comes home, and when you see how normal she is you realize t'was only a bad dream. Now have a cup of tea and stop yer worryin'."

Once Harold drank his tea he felt the need to get out of the house, his nerves frayed. He kept hoping it had only been a dream, but after Tannith's description he realized it was unlikely. For one thing he'd never even heard of this Gan Ceannach. How could he dream of him? And Maeve's face in his mind held an expression that had only ever been reserved for him. He ran along the path trying to let go of his panic. But in his heart he knew nothing could shake this until Maeve got back—if she ever did.

CHAPTER TEN

I reached Tiadan late morning of the next day. The night before I'd hardly slept at all, my senses on alert for the return of Gan Ceanach or a showdown with the flock of ravens that still followed me. By the time I reached Tannith's house I was frantic with worry. I couldn't imagine telling Harold what I'd done, and even worse, I couldn't get the love talker out of my mind. And Harold knew me well enough to know when I was hiding something. What was the faery's plan, anyway? Just make love to me so that I was under his power and then disappear leaving me to completely freak out? That was pretty much the exact scenario Rea had warned me about. Gan Ceanach had said this was about the ravens but barely mentioned them, instead ravishing me and then leaving without a backward glance.

When I reached the house Tannith hurried out to take the baby from me. "Harold is workin' on your house today; ye will be surprised to see how far along it is."

"I'll take Pooka to the stables," I told her, trying to conjure the joy I usually felt before seeing Harold. But my only thoughts were on Gan Ceanach and when I could see him again. Once I led Pooka down the hill and pulled off the saddle and bridle, I put my mind on what I would say to Harold. He would be sure to ask me questions. "Do you have any advice for me?" I whispered in Pooka's ear.

Pooka turned his head and I was sure he knew exactly what I was talking about, but he didn't answer. I turned him loose. He was a magical creature and bonded to me. I only wished his connection with the Fae could help in my current predicament.

After feeding the baby and having a cup of tea and some bread and cheese, I rose from my place at the table. "I'll go see Harold now," I said, a heaviness descending onto my shoulders.

When Tannith turned from where she worked her cheeses I was sure she heard the reluctance in my voice. "Why don't you leave the baby here with me?" she asked, misinterpreting my tone for exhaustion. "I have nothin' much to attend to and you dinna need to carry her such a long way. Ye will be back before her next feeding?"

I nodded, trying to smile. "I won't be long."

By now the day had turned overcast and cold, matching my mood. I pulled on my wool cloak and headed out the door. Along the main path to the village I found the trail that led to the secluded hill where Harold had chosen to build. It was nice not to have to worry about boundaries and right-of-ways and paying for land. Here the land was freely given and shared among all residents. I wished I could feel excitement about the prospect of sharing a house with Harold, but all I could think about was the faery. When would I see him again?

Before I reached the last rise I heard the bang of hammers, the sound of laughter and men's voices. The framework came into view, the logs newly sawn. If the snows held off it wouldn't be many days before we could move in. The sea shone dark in the distance, a mist rising off the water. I knew it was a beautiful scene, but I couldn't appreciate it at all.

"Maeve!" I heard Harold shout. A second later he was running toward me. When he reached me he picked me up and twirled me around in his arms. "God, I've missed you!"

"It was only a little over a week," I grumbled, trying to wriggle free.

He put me on the ground and stared hard into my eyes. "What's happened?"

When I met those moss-colored eyes my own filled with tears. "I have a lot to tell you," I said.

When he bent to kiss me I turned away. "The men are watching us," I said.

He pulled back, frowning. "Since when did you care about that?"

I shrugged. "Let's wait till later, okay?"

He put his arm around my shoulders to walk up the hill. "Where's Airy?"

"I left her with Tannith."

"We need to cut more logs in order to go on; I think I'll call it a day."

"But Harold, you—"

He turned to me in surprise. "Don't you want to spend time with me?" He lifted one eyebrow. "I have plans for you, milady."

"Of course I do, it's just—" I pointed ineffectually at the five men still working. "What about them?"

73

"I'll see you all here tomorrow!" Harold yelled. "My lady's back."

A cheer went up and then the group moved to put away tools. I recognized a few of them from when Harold led them as Kenneth; they had fought together, sheltered together, buried the dead together. Once the men headed away Harold took my hand and proudly showed off what they'd accomplished. The floors were packed earth, the walls done with post and beam construction. It was perfect in every way, and yet I couldn't feel joy about it.

"What's wrong, Maeve?"

"I just have a lot on my mind."

"I have a remedy for that."

"But the baby is at home, and—"

"There's always the stable for privacy," he said, pulling me after him down the hill. As I hurried with him back toward Tannith's cottage I tried to come up with reasons why this wasn't a good idea—I could get pregnant—not true since I was still breast-feeding—I didn't feel well—also not true and he would know better.

By the time we reached the stable and he'd led the way inside I was out of excuses. If I put him off I would have to explain why, and I wasn't ready for that. I loved him—what was my problem? My problem was that I had somehow been taken over by Fae magic. In reality I felt nothing for Harold and had no interest in having sex with him.

Harold undid my cloak and pulled it off, his hands roving across my body and tugging at my clothes. I closed my eyes and tried to enjoy it, but by the time we were stretched out in the hay I was crying, tears flowing out of my eyes like I'd lost my best friend. And maybe I had.

Harold pulled back to stare at me. "Maeve, what in hell is going on with you? We haven't had sex in over five months—I expected you to be all over me. Why are you crying?"

"Something happened while I was gone—" I began, trying to find an excuse that would make sense without telling him the truth.

He frowned. "Something that won't wait until after we've reconnected?"

"The ravens," I blurted. "The ravens have been bewitched again. They were following me. I wanted to tell you what I was feeling before I left, but I didn't want to worry you."

Harold rested on his elbows, staring down with dark eyes. "You knew about this before you left for the celebration and you didn't tell me?"

I pushed myself up to sitting and pulled my dress down. "I didn't know about the ravens then, but I've had strange premonitions for several months now."

"Premonitions—if that means what I think it does you had no business going off alone with our baby. Why didn't you tell me?"

"I didn't want Kenneth to come to the rescue. I wanted to let it play out and talk with MacCuill before I told you."

Harold pushed himself up, his eyes narrowing. "And what did the all-powerful druid say?"

I ignored the snide comment. "He hadn't heard anything, but Gunnar was there and said something very different."

"Gunnar? Have I met him?"

"Maybe not—he says he will know Airy when she's older."

Harold ran his hands through his thick hair. "Well, that's helpful." He watched me with his head cocked to one side. "What aren't you saying?"

Heat rushed into my cheeks, but before I could answer I heard the unmistakable whoosh of winged creatures. I rose hurriedly and moved to the door, Harold right behind me. The sky was dark enough that I couldn't see them well, but it had to be the ravens, and this time there were so many the sky was black with them.

"What's going on?" Harold muttered, stepping out. A second later he was dive-bombed, and when he backed up his cheek was bleeding, a long scratch on his forearm. He slammed the barn door closed. "What the hell?" His wide eyes met mine.

"I don't know. Gan Ceanach said—" I put my hand to my mouth.

Harold grabbed my arm, spinning me to face him. "Gan Ceanach, the love talker?"

"You've heard of him? He's one of the Fae."

Harold folded his arms across his chest, his eyes glittering in the semi-darkness of the barn. "Tannith told me all about him. I had a dream about you and him, Maeve. What happened between you two?"

I opened my mouth and closed it, looking away. The birds still circled, waiting for us to emerge. "He said that Morrighan is involved with the ravens. He wants my help to go against her."

"Your help? Why not MacCuill, or this other druid, Gunnar? What about the gods and goddesses? You have a baby now; you're in no position to go off in battle mode to fight the goddess of war."

I let out a long sigh. "He never explained what he had in mind."

"Jesus, Maeve. I should have gone with you. Those birds are not in their right minds. You're lucky you didn't get hurt or killed on the way home. And my gods--Airy was with you!" He grabbed my arm, pinching it painfully. "Now tell me what happened between you two; did he kiss you?"

I stared at him, unable to answer.

Harold let go of my arm. "Answer me, Maeve," he said in a tone that scared me.

"I—he—"

"He what?" he asked, grabbing me by the shoulders. "Did he do more than kiss you? If he did you've been bewitched; do you realize that? Did he stay with you overnight? What exactly happened between the two of you?" He was shouting now, his face red and furious.

I didn't answer as I gathered up my cloak and slipped it around my shoulders. "I'm sure Airy is screaming with hunger by now," I said. "How do we get from here to the house?"

Harold scowled at me before he opened the door to take a look. "They've moved on. Follow me," he ordered, hurrying up the hill.

By the time we reached the house I was crying again. Harold's face was a mask, his eyes unreadable. He strode through the door ahead of me and went up to our room, taking the stairs two at a time. I heard his boots clomping about over our heads, the thump as he threw them off.

"What has got into Harold?" Tannith asked, handing over a red-faced Airy. "And why are ye crying? What has happened between ye?"

When I sat at the table to feed her, Airy turned away from the breast, a scowl appearing on her already red face. She let out a howl and began to cry in earnest. I shook my head and tried to send loving thoughts her way, but there was no love inside me for anything or anyone but Gan Ceanach. I had to get out from under the spell or Harold and I were doomed. And yet I didn't want to.

Tannith didn't question me further as she wrapped up her cheeses and left the house. "I'll be back later," she said from the doorway. "I'll give the two of ye some privacy to make amends." The door banged closed behind her leaving me alone with my thoughts. Meanwhile Airy would have nothing to do with me.

The idea of a real showdown with Harold made me cringe. I couldn't spell out what had happened--it would hurt him too much. And besides, he already knew without me telling him. I placed the screaming baby in the papoose I'd left on a chair by the door, pulled my cloak on and left the house.

"Pooka," I called in a hushed whisper once I reached the Yew forest. He appeared a moment later, gazing at me from intelligent eyes. "You need to use all your magic to keep us safe," I told him, pulling myself up on his wide back. "Take me to Gan Ceanach."

The horse gave me a look that seemed filled with anxiety, and I swear he shook his head, but once I was on his back he led the way through the Yew forest and down the hill on the other side. As we got further away from Tiadan my tears began again, my sobs echoing into the distance. I felt split apart, as though my body would just break in half. But under it I felt desperate to see Gan Ceanach. I had to find him.

As I rode I was so psychically exhausted that I actually fell asleep, my head bouncing against Pooka's thick mane, his movements smooth like that of a gaited horse. I had no idea where the horse was taking me until I woke up on the outskirts of Caer Sidi. In the distance the eastern hardwood forests lay like a dark smudge against a sky suffused with moonlight. I was pretty sure Gan Ceanach would not be anywhere near here.

I slid off the horse. "Why did you bring me here, Pooka? I specifically told you to find Gan Ceanach." He wouldn't meet my eyes, but inclined his head as though pointing. I turned, hoping to see the love talker, but instead it was Duncan striding toward me.

"Maeve! What might ye be doin' here in the middle of the night? I thought you and yer man were buildin' a house."

"I—I didn't plan to come here. I told Pooka to take me—" I faltered, realizing that it wouldn't go over well to tell him the truth. "Is this where you live now?" I asked, trying to keep my tears from erupting and giving me away.

He nodded, gazing at me quizzically. "Maeve, what is wrong with ye? Ye seem distraught. Where is yer baby?"

"I left her...with Harold," I added, noticing his expression.

"Ye left her—? Are ye not still breast-feedin'?"

"It doesn't matter," I muttered. "Harold will take good care of her."

Duncan stared at me for a long moment. "Follow me," he finally said, heading under the low-lying branches of an enormous fig tree. "Ye look like ye could use a place to lay your head."

Under the limbs thick roots jutted up from the ground, a small doorway set back inside them. Duncan pulled aside a bough revealing a small door and slipped inside, waiting for me before pulling the door closed. A lantern hung on a protruding root, illuminating the unusual space. The inner part of the tree had been removed, leaving the cambium layer and the bark. Duncan had fashioned a bed and filled it with blankets of sheep's wool. On the other side of the roundish room a tiny fire pit had been dug and surrounded with river rocks. Above it hung several articles of cookware, and above that a hole had been drilled through to the outside to allow the smoke to escape. Duncan kneeled to add a few pieces to the smoldering fire, bringing it to a merry blaze. I watched the smoke drift up in a fine tendril. I began to cry, tears spilling down my cheeks before I could stop them.

Duncan stared at me. "What is it, lass?"

"Gan Ceanach," I said before I could stop myself.

"Ye've had contact with the Fae? They normally keep to themselves. Gan Ceanach is a slippery devil. Are ye saying you've met him?"

"Gan Ceannach wants me to help him go against Morrighan."

Duncan looked up, his expression shocked. "The love talker. Have ye had a run-in with the wee man, lass?"

I hung my head and he knew, his mouth dropping open. "Ye are obsessed with him now, is that it?"

"I can't get him out of my mind; it's like nothing else matters but seeing him, being with him again, and--"

"So, that's why ye left the wee bairn with Harold." Duncan's blue eyes narrowed with distress. "Ye must find a way to break the spell."

"I don't want to break the spell; I only want to find him. I love him, Duncan."

"Ye only think ye love him, lass. That's what he does. Ye will die of it, Maeve, if ye dinna break the spell he has over ye."

"But he said he wants my help to combat Morrighan. He told me she's bewitched the ravens and plans to take over Otherworld."

"I fear that's a lie. He used it to gain yer trust. I have heard nothing about Morrighan these past months, and as to the ravens, they are free from magic."

"No, they aren't. They nearly killed my baby when I was on the way to the dolmen. When I got back to Tiadan, two of them attacked Harold and drew blood."

"I think Gan Canach is stirring up trouble as the faeries are wont to do. Ye canna trust a word the man says. Maeve, why are ye here without yer man? Surely he wouldn't want ye traipsing all over Otherworld alone. Does he understand what has happened?"

I looked up and wiped the corners of my eyes. "I didn't tell Harold directly, but I'm sure he knows. Pooka brought me here. I asked him to take me to Gan Ceanach."

"The beastie can nay take ye to the wee man. Fairies are not wanderin' around the forest like human folk, especially now that he has done what he came for. He is more than likely off to possess another unsuspecting female who will drive herself insane trying to find him, just as you are."

I tried to ignore what he was saying. Surely Gan Ceanach was pledged to me just as I was to him. What we'd done together had hardly been a casual liaison. "I left thinking I would reconnect with Gan Ceanach—it's all I want right now, and—"

He held up his hand to stop me. "No more of this. First we have to find someone powerful enough to break the spell and then we need to deal with this nonsense about Morrighan and the ravens. I suggest a visit to the goddess of war. If ye ask her directly she will never lie."

I struggled with myself, trying to let go of the gnawing need to be with Gan Ceanach. I knew with certainty that the feelings weren't real, and yet— I even felt guilt for having told Duncan as much as I had. The faery would be angry if he knew what I'd divulged.

"Sleep now, Maeve," Duncan said, moving from where he sat on his bed. "I'll rest by the fire. In the mornin' I will ask around and find out who can break the spell."

I crawled into the small bed, imagining Gan Ceanach beside me. I fell asleep to the sound of the crackling flames, hoping my dreams would take me to the faery.

CHAPTER ELEVEN

Harold threw his boots against the wall, the thud they made not nearly satisfying enough. He wanted to smash his fist into something, but Tannith's wall would suffer if he let his anger out. He had a sick feeling in the pit of his stomach thinking about the expression on Maeve's face after she told him about the man. It was as if Harold no longer existed. Who was this Gan Ceanach? Right now he wanted to find the little fucker and kill him—was it even possible to kill a faery?

He pulled on his boots and stomped down the stairs, but when he reached the lower floor there was no one there but Airy. Her face was bright red and wet with tears where she lay inside the papoose by the door. Thankfully she'd cried herself to sleep. Where had Maeve gone without the baby? He picked up the papoose and ran outside to check along the cliff edge, but she wasn't there. It was then he heard Argyll neigh and headed down the hill to check on Pooka. The black horse was gone, as well as the saddle and bridle. Fury filled him, blood suffusing his eyeballs as he tried to get control of himself. He ran back to the house and threw open the door with one hand, holding on to the baby with the other. Pacing up and down he let his mind rush from one thing to the next, none of it very helpful.

When Tannith walked in the door her gaze went to the baby in his arms. "Where is Maeve?"

"I have no fucking idea!" he shouted. "She's probably looking for that little asshole—how could she leave the baby?" He smashed his fist against the door, bruising his knuckles in the process and obviously scaring Tannith.

"Harold—calm down!" she said, taking the sleeping baby out of his arms. "You aren't thinking straight and you'll wake Airy. Sit down and tell me what she said."

"I don't have time to sit down; the woman I love is out in some wilderness searching for the bastard who raped her."

"If you're talking about Gan Ceanach, he didn't rape her," Tannith said quietly, looking him in the eye. "The only way the spell works is if the woman is willing to—"

"To let him screw her?"

"Harold, enough with the language. Ye need to calm down and collect yourself. It isn't her fault--she's under a spell."

"But she left Airy—"

"I know," Tannith said, heading to a cupboard. She opened it with one hand and pulled out a dark bottle and then moved to the shelf by the sink where she collected two mugs. She poured amber liquid into both of them and handed him one. "Drink this and try and settle yourself. Rushing off in this kind of mood will do nothing to help her or you."

Harold slugged back the liquid and put his head between his hands. He couldn't believe this was happening.

"We need to find out what this man is up to and why he targeted Maeve. He must want her powers. There really isn't any other reason I can think of."

"Her powers? How would having sex with her give him her powers?"

"She is under his spell and that means he can tap into whatever she's capable of doing. From what I know of the Fae they have many abilities, but none as unique as the Willow."

"She said something about the ravens and then two of them attacked me. Are they connected with the Fae?"

Tannith shook her head. "Not that I know of, and I can't think of any reason why they would attack unless they are under a spell as well."

"Oh great—not again," Harold muttered. "I'll have to take Airy and go find her."

When he turned to put on his coat Tannith grabbed hold of his arm. "How do ye plan to feed her? Leave her here with me and I'll find a wet nurse. There are plenty of women with small bairns in town. And besides, I've heard stories about a group of Welsh faeries who run with Gan Ceanach and they've been known to kidnap babies."

Harold jerked his head up. "Are you serious?"

"I shouldn't have said anything, but taking Airy with you could put her in danger. And it would hinder your ability to travel quickly, even if you had the means to feed her."

"Why are the Fae here?" Harold asked again, his eyes welling.

"Otherworld was their home before the war and possibly they just want to return."

He shook his head, feeling dizzy for a second. "I think it's more than that and I'm going to find out."

A knock at the door startled both of them, their eyes meeting before Tannith moved to open it. "I was wonderin' where the boss man is," Dougal began before his gaze landed on Harold's distraught expression. "What in hell has happened?" he asked.

"Maeve left me," Harold mumbled, pouring more whiskey in his glass.

"Maeve has been bewitched by a faery," Tannith clarified. "She's gone off to find him."

"Holy gods," Dougal gasped. "Are ye speakin' of the one they call the 'love talker'?"

"That's the one," Harold answered, knocking back the whiskey and pouring more. He tipped it up and drank it down in one gulp. "What do you know about him?"

"I know he's no one to mess with. The only way ye can break the spell is to find a witch."

Harold stared at his friend, his eyes dark and angry. "Do you know of one? Because if you don't, I suggest you get the hell out of here." He slammed his glass down on the table and poured more whiskey into it.

Dougal didn't react, his gaze going to the baby in Tannith's arms. "Harold, I've known ye for a while now and I've seen yer moods. If ye dinna want my help I'll leave."

"Don't go," Tannith said quickly. "Harold needs you even if he says he doesn't. Do you have any idea where we might find a witch?"

"I don't personally, but I have a lot of friends in this town. I'm certain I can turn up someone who's had dealings with a witch or two. Trust me Harold, we'll get her back. But what do ye plan to do with the wee one?"

By that time Harold was feeling the effects of the eighty-proof scotch on an empty stomach. He sat heavily and stared at Dougal. "I don't know." He looked up at Tannith. "What do you suggest?"

"I'll check in town and employ one of the women who have recently given birth. It won't be difficult to find a wet nurse."

A second later Airy woke and began to wail, her piteous cries angering Harold further. "How could she leave our baby behind? I thought she loved her."

"She's not in her right mind," Tannith said, rocking Airy. "But be happy she did, Harold. Ye wouldn't want Airy out there in the forest with a woman who can barely take care of herself. I'm takin' Airy into town to find a wet nurse."

"My woman is feedin' our wee one," Dougal said. "And by the look of it she has enough milk for an army."

Tannith carried the screaming baby with her out the door. "Do what ye need, Harold," she called over her shoulder. "Airy will be fine with Breena."

Dougal sat at the table, his gaze trained on Harold. "Where do you think Maeve would go?"

Harold shrugged. "If she's trying to find this faery I have no idea."

"I say the two of us comb the woods between here and Caer Sidi. If we canna find her we gather a search party."

Having a plan galvanized Harold's scattered state of mind. Less than an hour later the two men were on horseback heading for the forest. In Harold's agitated state he let Dougal take over as he attempted to control his fury and wild thoughts. His hand was on his sword and he itched to drive the blade deep into Gan Ceanach's chest.

They'd been searching methodically when Harold pulled Argyll to a stop. "Why are there no tracks? Where could she have gone?"

"I don't know, but night falls early these days. I think we should ride hard for Caer Sidi and organize a search party."

Harold nodded, unable to think of a better idea.

CHAPTER TWELVE

I woke with a start, my thoughts as always going to Gan Ceanach. I'd been with him only a moment before in my dream.

"Ah, you're awake."

I grimaced, looking up at Duncan. "And I wish I wasn't." I had to express some milk, but to do so I would need privacy.

"Have some bannock and then we can talk with Rea. She might have some idea about a witch."

I swung my legs off the bed. "I already told you, I don't want to find a witch—I want to find Gan Ceanach."

"Maeve, ye are not thinkin' clearly."

I headed toward the tiny door. "Right now I have to do my morning ritual, Duncan. Please leave me to it."

Duncan watched me with a worried expression. "Will Harold come?"

"I hope not," I said, pulling the door closed behind me. I headed into the woods behind Duncan's tree house to relieve myself. After that I dealt with the excess milk. Hopefully it would dry up soon. I had no wish or reason to be lactating.

When I returned to Duncan's shelter he was gone. I settled on the bed and fell asleep again, my dreams taking me to Gan Ceanach. *"Why won't you come back to me?" I asked from where I lay naked on soft moss.*

"I'm with you now, isn't that enough?" He bent to place his beautiful mouth on mine and I pulled him to me. But before we'd had a chance to complete what we'd begun Duncan's arrival woke me. "Damn it!" I yelled, watching Gan Ceanach recede into dreamy wisps.

"Maeve, what is it?" he asked, hurrying to the bed.

"Nothing." I turned away, trying to bring my aroused body back to some normalcy.

"Ye need to get yourself under control, lass," Duncan said, watching me. "Ye have a baby and a man who loves ye. Don't throw it away over this Fae who is only usin' ye."

I opened my mouth to argue that Gan Ceanach wasn't using me, but I didn't care whether he was or wasn't. I only knew that I wanted him more than I'd wanted anything in my life.

When I laid my head down to go to sleep again Duncan came and shook me by the shoulder. "No more dreamin' for ye, lass. Rea will be here any minute, and if I know her she will be draggin' ye up and out of here to figure out a solution to this mess."

"You told her what was going on?"

"I did, and she knows of this Gan Ceanach character. She's a spitfire, that one."

Yes she was, and right now I didn't want to deal with it. "Can you tell her I'm sick or something?" I whined, staring at Duncan.

"Not on yer life. Ye need her now more than ever."

It was sometime later that there was a tentative knock on the door. Duncan admitted the diminutive woman with the upturned eyes and took that moment to exit. "I'll leave ye to it," he said.

When my gaze met Rea's I had to turn away.

"I hear you are under the love talker's nasty spell," she said, sitting next to me. "Duncan tells me you are not interested in mothering your child, that you left her behind. Is that true?"

I nodded, still unable to meet her amber eyes.

"It is a witch you need to break the spell," she said matter-of-factly. "But I have seen no witches in Otherworld for many a year. How did this come about? I thought you were smarter than this."

I looked up, angry. "He found me in the forest and he kissed me. I need him. I'll die if I don't see him. I love him."

Rea lowered her gaze. "You *think* you love him, Maeve. He is an evil fairy who cares nothing for you."

"That isn't true! He—"

Rea held up her small hand. "Years ago one of my people had a run-in with him. She died. I told you all this at the dolmen. Do you not remember?"

"But—"

"Have you lost your memory too? She gave birth to a faery baby and abandoned the wee one in favor of finding the father."

"What happened to the baby?" I asked, wondering if I could be carrying Gan Ceanach's child.

"The clan raised him, but once he was two years of age the faeries took him back. By that time Clen had died of starvation from her constant search for Gan Ceanach. You see you are one of many, and not special to him at all."

"I don't believe you."

Rea waited a moment before continuing. "He takes what he wants and those he touches are in his thrall. In your case he may want something more. If you see him again you will surely find out."

"I hope I see him again," I whispered to myself.

"I have spoken to a druid friend and a few others to find a witch to break this spell. Duncan will keep you safe until we have alerted Harold."

I watched her leave and a few minutes later I rose from the bed. I had to be gone when Harold arrived. I would find Gan Ceanach or die trying, I thought, exiting the tiny house.

Instead of calling my horse I headed into the woods on foot. Pooka was no longer trustworthy. After the dream I was sure Gan Ceanach would find me if I made myself available to him.

Halfway up the trail I realized I was barefoot, my feet freezing cold and bleeding from the rocks and pebbles I was climbing over. When the trail abruptly ended I moved under the trees, letting my intuition tell me where to go. I was the Willow and I'd faced much worse obstacles than finding a faery. As far as my feet and the snow that had just begun to fall, I could take it.

I wasn't sure how much time had gone by when I became aware that the meager light had leached from the sky. It was night and I was lost in a part of the forest I'd never been before. The snow had been falling steadily for hours and lay in heavy drifts against the trees and boulders. When I looked down my feet were blue against the white and I couldn't feel them. My dress was soaked through and I realized I was shivering violently. No matter, I thought, moving forward. I would rest when it was time. He would find me before I froze to death. I smiled to myself at the thought of his face, his perfect body, and his arms tight around me. I opened my mouth to the snow, letting the cold flakes land on my tongue. They tasted sweet just as Gan Ceanach did. I sent my thoughts out to him, calling him in my mind. He would find me.

There came a point at which I was unable to move anymore. I hadn't eaten in a day and a half, my breasts were full again and my feet burned as though on fire. I found a spot under a tree and managed to express some milk before curling into a ball, trying to stay warm.

Gan Ceanach—Gan Ceanach—I called out. *Please come to me. I need you.* I heard him before I saw him, his dark form appearing within a mist so soupy that I could barely make him out.

When he came to stand next to me I reached out for him, but he only stared. "Before we go further you must give me your powers. If you do not I will not make love to you, nor will I keep you warm through this freezing night. You will be dead by morning."

"Anything you want, my love," I answered, trying to reach his hand.

"Take off your clothes," he ordered.

When I pulled the dress over my head, the shaking grew worse, but I told myself that he would soon be next to me, and his Fae magic would warm me. He knelt, his normally golden eyes dark as he placed his palms on each side of my head. "Give me your magic, Maeve—I want all of it. Do it quickly before your mind goes numb from exposure."

"Will you love me after?"

He nodded, his palms pressing against my head. "If you do not give me everything, I will know, and I will leave you here to die."

His touch created an aching need that I could barely tolerate, my mind hurtling forward to the feel of his sweet mouth on mine. "But don't the Fae have all that magic?"

"Not anymore," he replied impatiently. "Do you want me to make love to you?"

"Yes, yes, I'll do anything, Gan Ceanach." I ignored the shaking in my body, the feeling that my feet were no longer part of me. I focused on his fingers digging into my temples, his forehead pressed against mine. "This is like a Vulcan mind meld," I giggled, but he didn't respond.

A moment later I felt a steady stream of some wisps of memory leaving me.

"I want the healing, the ability to move through the ether, the clairvoyance. All of it."

I concentrated on those things, imagining them going from my mind into his. I remembered how it felt the first time I was able to heal, the first time I'd moved from one place to another just by thinking about it. I felt the faery pulling my magic, sliding it out of me, and I helped it along, knowing that as soon as he had what he wanted he would make love to me. The odd and unpleasant draining sensation went on for a long time before Gan Ceanach stood. I lifted my face to his, reaching up with both hands.

His mouth curled into an unpleasant grin. "Thank you," he said. And a second later he used what I'd given him, disappearing in front of my eyes.

"No!" I shouted. "Come back! I need you!" But my hoarse voice was lost inside the thick white that blanketed the forest. I pulled my knees up, hugging them as my body and my mind registered what he'd done. I felt drained and sick, weak with longing as well as the sense that I was no longer truly alive, my essential essence gone.

There was no sound and no sign of him as the snow continued to fall, piling up around my bare feet and legs. And when I searched for my clothes I couldn't find them. I curled into a ball, tears freezing on my cheeks. This was what he'd wanted all along. Without him I wanted to die, and this wish would more than likely be granted very soon.

CHAPTER THIRTEEN

"With any luck we'll be in Caer Sidi by tonight," Dougal said, turning in the saddle. His sturdy pony was small in comparison with Argyll, and more nimble because of it.

But unfortunately luck was not with them, and when snow began to fall the track grew treacherous. It was hours of riding along narrow paths slick with mud and ice before the thickly treed area began to open up. Coming out from under the trees brought with it an ice-filled wind from which there was no longer any protection. Clouds drifted by, moonlight illuminating the valley spread before them like a blanket meant for a giant. In the far distance the sea lay gray and still as though the snow had covered it with an entirely different substance. The ghostly landscape was pristine and beautiful, but Harold could take no pleasure in it.

When they reached the river they pushed the horses north along the bank until they located the bridge. The planks were so slick they had to dismount to cross and still Harold was sure Argyll would go down.   But the piebald managed without mishap. On the other side Dougal went ahead, pushing his horse toward the meandering trail leading to the thousand-foot hill in the distance. It was hours before they reached the top, the horses slick with sweat despite the cold. The view of the valley on the far side reminded Harold of those last few days before the end of the war—the chaos of clashing swords, screams of pain and death taking place across the valley floor. He tried to shake the foreboding away, but his exhaustion, the lack of food, and stress had taken their toll.

Now that the war was over no guards patrolled the border to the sacred realm. The land stretched away, hillocks and small valleys undulating toward the sea in the far distance. When the moon disappeared behind clouds the hills became black shapes that resembled sleeping dragons. This was the most sacred part of Otherworld, where the moon goddess had her castle, where the queen of the druids lived in a gigantic monolith made of red stone. The energy here was kept pure by the many tribes who peopled it, and it shimmered, a pale glittering mist that lay along the land's surface.

MacCuill's cottage came into view, the whitewashed stone in a hollow between two low hills. No smoke emerged from the chimney; the druid was away. Duncan's tree house lay to the north and east, close to where the festival had been held and where Maeve had given birth to their baby girl. Harold had spent time there drinking with Duncan during Maeve's long labor. His anger was long gone now, his heart contracting with worry as her face appeared in his mind. By tomorrow they would have a group together to search. He pressed his legs against the horse, moving forward through the snow to pass by Dougal.

"Where are ye headed?" Dougal asked.

"Duncan's seems the best bet. He won't mind being awakened in the middle of the night, especially if it has to do with the Willow."

Dougal nodded. "You are right about that."

It was another hour of hard riding before they arrived at the spot reserved for festivals. Duncan's tree house wasn't far. Harold dismounted and pulled the saddle and bridle off. "Go forage, big guy, and try to stay warm," he murmured in his ear. He loved Argyll fiercely and the horse knew it. The piebald gave him a look and then trotted away, moving under the trees where some grass still poked through. Harold pulled his deerskin coat closer, very glad to have it. That and the heavy boots he wore were the only things keeping him warm. This was the first snow since the end of the war. The weather had been gray and cold during those awful months but no moisture had fallen, what little water there was coming from a couple of springs and a stream or two. He had to say that despite the inconvenience, the snow was welcome when compared to the dismal desolation of the last winter. He turned when he heard Dougal behind him.

"I hope there's some grass for them. That was more than I've put that pony through since the war."

"They'll be fine. The grass is thick under the snow."

A moment later Duncan appeared. "Thought I heard someone out here."

"We came to enlist your help," Harold began, turning to Dougal.

"Come in out of the cold. I'll fix ye both a cup of tea."

"I think we need something stronger than that," Harold said, stamping his feet to get the snow off. "We've been searching for Maeve all day and half the night."

Duncan led the way inside and went to the shelf. "Is this what ye're thinkin' of?" he asked, holding up a bottle of whiskey.

"That'll do," Harold said. He moved close to the fire and held his hands out to the warmth.

"Maeve was here but she took off. I followed her tracks but it was snowin' too hard and I lost them. Bad thing is she's barefoot and without her cloak."

Harold swiveled to stare at him. "She took off barefoot without Pooka?"

"Ye have to realize she's besotted, Harold. This is Fae magic and canna be broken without help." Duncan turned to the pot that already held tea and poured it into two mugs. He added a good amount of whiskey to each cup. "This should fix ye up until you get some bread and cheese into your gullets." He reached for a loaf of bread and a square of cheese, arranging them on a wooden plate.

Harold took a sip. "Will you be part of our search party?"

Duncan nodded, his eyes glazed with tears. "I have been through a war with the Willow and seein' her this way has hit me hard. I would have gone already but I didn't know which way to go—could have been me out there lost as well." He gave a humorless chuckle. "Not a good time to be wanderin' about the forest. Ye can be sure the faery will nae take care of her."

Harold slugged down his tea. "I have to find her," he said, putting his cup down. "She could freeze to death out there."

Duncan tried to smile. "Maeve is strong and she has magic. 'Twill be mornin' soon and we can enlist Rea's help. Have ye two spoken to the druid?"

"He wasn't at his cottage."

"He's moved into the castle. Ye'll find him there."

"Why is Rea still here? Last I heard she was living back in her home in the tunnels."

"She and a small group of Crion have come to make sure all is well in Caer Sidi. I suppose Maeve's warnings have rippled through Otherworld by now."

Harold put his hand on the door handle. "I can't sit here with the knowledge that's she out in a snow storm. I should be back by morning. If I'm not, send out a search party."

Dougal reached for his coat. "I'm coming with you."

"No. You stay here and get some sleep. That way at least one of us will have his faculties."

"If ye find her and she's seriously gone I would suggest takin' her to the healing spring," Duncan warned.

Harold grimaced. "I hope it won't come to that. Can the healing goddess help with the spell?"

Duncan shook his head.

Harold's nerves felt like taut wires that might twang apart at any moment. His stomach roiled from the strong tea laced with whiskey he'd drunk, his mind filled with visions of Maeve lying dead in the snow. He remembered this morning as though it was another lifetime. Could this really be the same day? He pulled on his coat. "I'll see you both in a couple of hours."

Harold was on the piebald about to enter the forest when he heard someone call his name. He turned to see Rea hurrying

101

toward him, a cloak pulled over her copper hair. Did everyone here stay up all night?

"I can't stay, Rea. I have to find Maeve."

Rea grabbed hold of the reins. "The spell she's under is a strong one, Harold. MacCuill has alerted the druids and they are all searching for a way to break the magic."

"I'm glad to hear that, but right now I've got to go. She could be anywhere, and if I don't find her, she…"

Rea let go and backed away. "If anyone can locate her it is you. But I must caution you that she is not in her right mind. Do not take how she behaves to heart."

"Right now I'm just worried that she's out there freezing to death." He put his hand up in a wave and kicked Argyll under the trees. It was still very dark and difficult to see any tracks without dismounting to search. He kneeled in the snow every thirty of forty feet, scouting the area for prints before remounting to continue. It was methodical and tedious and he tried to let his mind float free, attempting to connect with her. They had always been linked—why would now be any different?

An hour later Harold was in deep woods following a non-existent path that led nowhere. He gave Argyll his head, allowing the horse to make the decisions about which drifts to avoid and how to get around the thickly clumped trees and boulders that hid under a layer of snow. He felt nearly delirious with exhaustion and worry, and couldn't for the life of him connect with any intuition he might once have had. All bets were off when he was tracking Maeve, especially with temperatures lowering into the single digits. He pulled his coat closer, shivering as a lump of snow fell from the tree branches, landing inside his collar. He urged the horse on, pushing him into an uneven trot through the deep drifts.

It was hours of this before his eyes began to droop, lack of sleep and taut nerves drawing him into a stupor. At one point he nearly fell off, waking just in time.

When Argyll came to an abrupt stop he tumbled forward and slid off, too tired to try and stay in the saddle. By now the snow had let up; there was a stillness amongst the enormous trees that felt almost reverent. It was dark and yet the layer of white brightened the forest, sparkling as though a distant light was shining on it.

He was about to remount when he noticed a woman's bare footprints in the snow, a stain of blood streaked across the indented white. He left Argyll and followed the prints up a small hill and down the other side. He went on like this for some time until the print trail ended. "Maeve!" he called out, but the only answer was the hiss of wind and the light dusting of snow that cascaded down like grains of sugar from the branches overhead. He walked in a circle, attempting to find the prints again, but the more he searched the more he messed up whatever prints there may have been. It was simply too dark. He finally sat on the ground with his back against a tree and closed his eyes. Just a few minutes he thought—*just enough rest so that I can think clearly.*

Chapter Fourteen

I heard a voice but couldn't open my eyes. I realized with a start that they were frozen shut. When I tried to move my arm to wipe the ice away it seemed stuck to my side. Was I dead? I certainly felt dead, my body numb and shaking, as though I had no control over it. My mind was empty as though evil winds had scooped it out. I knew with a certainty that I was no longer the Willow. I was now merely Maeve Lewin from Milltown, a young, not very interesting woman who had experienced greatness. Gan Ceanach had promised— he'd told me he would love me if I gave him what he asked for, and yet he went away without even kissing me. I thought faeries had to tell the truth. Tears formed and pressed through my iced lashes, melting them before freezing again. My teeth chattered so hard I thought they would crack apart. I welcomed my coming death. What was the point of living without Gan Ceanach?

The past rolled by in varying shades of gray. My life had been nothing before I met Gan Ceanach; even my baby held no interest now. I wanted him in a way I'd never felt before. I let out a small scream and called his name, but after that I began to drift. I no longer felt the cold, drowsiness taking me into an embrace that felt secure and soft, like a mother gathering me into her lap. A long time later I saw him in my mind, his face bending over me, his arms lifting me, but I was losing consciousness by that time, and could no longer respond.

Harold woke with a start wondering how long he'd been asleep. The sky had lightened slightly, although it was hard to tell in the gloom of the forest. He listened, sure he'd heard something, but there was nothing but the groan of limbs rubbing against one another. He pushed himself to standing and brushed the snow off. He was shaking with cold, his fingers numb inside the gloves he'd thought to wear. His toes felt like they were made of ice. And then he remembered Maeve with bare feet and no coat and let out a moan.

Argyll had found him, the big horse standing next to him with the saddle and bridle on. "I'm sorry big guy," he muttered, placing his hand on the wide neck. "You must have had as bad a night as I did." He remounted and pushed the horse toward where he'd last seen the footprints, hoping that Argyll would know how to find her. Why hadn't he thought to bring Pooka along? The magical creature would have led him directly to her. As though summoned, Pooka appeared, his nicker such a welcome sound that Harold let out a laugh. "What do you do now—materialize when someone thinks about you?" He stared into the golden eyes. "Find Maeve," he said, feeling a little bit idiotic, but the horse turned and trotted away, following a snowy trail up a small rise. Harold and Argyll followed.

It was another hour of walking before Harold noticed the footprints again. And when they came upon the still form beneath a tree, Harold was off his horse and running.

Maeve was completely naked, her skin blue and ice cold. Her hair had frozen around her face, sticking to the skin of her neck and shoulders. When he felt for a pulse it was faint and thready. Ice had frozen on her face, giving her cheeks an odd shiny look. Her eyelashes were frozen shut. He pressed his lips there, blowing gently until they began to thaw. When he lifted her, she felt insubstantial, her skin taut over the bones of her face. Instead of putting her on Pooka's back he wrapped her in his warm coat and held her in front of the saddle, attempting to warm her as he rode. It was hard going and he nearly lost her a couple of times before he thought to remove his belt and tie it around both of them. Luckily it had been woven in Otherworld and doubled as a rope when it needed to.

With her tied to him and one arm round her to keep her shoulders from slumping forward, he retraced his steps. When she moaned he took it for a good sign, but he knew if he didn't get her warm soon there would be no way of saving her. And as luck would have it the snow began again, and this time the wind came along with it. Snow blinded him, whirling from every direction. He had to stop. Without his coat his shirt was immediately drenched, his hair dripping ice down his back. If he weren't careful they would both die of hypothermia.

He slid off and pulled her with him, carrying her as he searched for a hollow or a shallow cave--anywhere to get out of the wind. But Pooka was already one step ahead, nosing him along toward a small hollow dug in beneath an enormous beech tree. He crawled inside, pulling her limp body after him. Once they were out of the wind he took off his wet clothes and pulled her close, covering them both with his heavy coat. He dozed then, exhausted from the ride, all adrenaline spent.

I felt Gan Ceanach against my body and knew he had finally come back to make love to me. I tried to open my eyes but they refused to cooperate. No matter, I thought, snuggling into him. He had warmed me up with his magic and brought me back from the dead. I moved against him trying to let him know I wanted him. At first he ignored it, and then he seemed to wake up, returning my caresses with ones of his own. "Oh," I murmured, my hands sliding across his skin. He felt hot under my fingers. "You came back," I murmured, my lips somehow finding his. His full mouth opened, his tongue searching. And when we connected it was like two sides of the same coin. I rocked against him, moaning as he took me, his rhythmic pulsing bringing me up to the brink and over. I felt him shudder, the low groan that escaped his lips. No more would I have to call his name and cry out for him. He was mine now. I fell asleep in his strong arms, my body warmed as well as my aching heart.

Harold woke suddenly, realizing that Maeve was pressing against him as though she wanted to make love. But how could this be? He'd found her near death only a few hours before. Her eyes were still squeezed shut, but the sounds she was making definitely indicated her intentions, that and her hands that roamed across his body, bringing him to life. At first he resisted, knowing what she'd been through and wondering how she could even have the energy for this. But he hadn't had sex for a very long time and his body had ideas of its own. When he returned her overtures, her movements became even more amorous, letting him know that she was serious about this. All his worries disappeared as he became a willing and eager partner, his thoughts lost inside the sensations and the connection between them. She loved him as she always had, the spell somehow broken. The love he felt for her brought tears of joy to his eyes as they became one, moving together as they always had, their bodies made for each other. And when they both lay spent he pulled her to him, murmuring his love into her hair as she snuggled against him. He adjusted his warm coat over them and fell asleep with his arms tight around her.

Chapter Fifteen

I woke with a start, realizing that what I thought had been a dream was actually true. Gan Ceanach was lying next to me keeping me warm, a sweep of dark hair across his cheek. He had saved my life. I was reaching over to give him a kiss when he turned, his face not the one I'd been expecting. "Harold? How did you get here?" I backed away.

He stared at me with a puzzled look. "You were happy enough to have me here last night."

"Last night—but I thought—" I looked around wildly and then felt the icy chill on my bare skin blowing in from the narrow opening. I gathered my arms around my body as Harold rose to his knees and placed his coat around my shoulders. He was naked.

He reached for his jeans. "I found you," he said, his eyes narrowing. "I thought you might die. There was a blizzard and I brought you here, and then you—"

"I what? Are you saying I seduced you last night?"

"I wouldn't exactly calling it seducing since I was an extremely willing partner." He grinned. "I think it's what saved you."

I shook my head, unable to fathom that the man I'd taken to be Gan Ceanach was actually Harold. I didn't want him here. "Go away."

"You're wearing my coat, Maeve. And other than that you have no clothes. You want to explain how that happened?"

I scanned back to my encounter with Gan Ceanach. He'd ordered me to take off my clothes, which I assumed was so we could make love. "Not really."

"Are you waiting for your lover to return, is that it? Because he won't be coming back."

"How do *you* know?" I asked huffily.

"I know all about Gan Ceanach now. He tried to kill you, Maeve. He left you naked in a blizzard. Does that sound like someone who cares?"

I stared at him, my anger growing stronger the more he talked. "Leave me alone, Harold. I don't love you. I want nothing to do with you. Gan Ceanach will be back; he must have had some business to attend to, that's all."

Harold shook his head. "I thought you'd come out from under his spell, but I guess I was wrong. It certainly seemed like that from the way you—"

"Don't say it!" I shrieked. "I don't care about you or anyone but Gan Ceanach! I mean it Harold. I want you to go away!"

Harold pulled on his wool shirt and his boots and then whistled for Argyll. "I'll leave Pooka here to take care of you, but if you don't get some warm food and some clothes you'll freeze to death."

"Take your damn coat," I said, flinging it at him as he pushed out of the hollow and strode away. But he didn't turn. A minute later he was on Argyll's back and I watched him disappear into the shadowy forest.

After he left I pulled my arms through his coat and huddled down to take stock. I needed sustenance; my belly was pulling in on itself, my muscles weak and tired. And without any of my powers I was nearly as vulnerable as a newborn babe. I had to find the faery or I would die of love. I crawled out and whistled to Pooka.

As I rode I racked my brain for some way to locate the faery. There had to be someone who would know how to reach him—a goddess perhaps, or another faery? But where had the Fae come from, where did they live? I couldn't ask any of the people I normally hung out with; they were all loyal to Harold. And then I remembered the underworld and Ceriddwen. She would know.

I rode all day trying to find the entrance to Ceriddwen's realm. It lay along the mountain range somewhere. The trails went up and down, narrowing and widening, all maddeningly familiar, but still I couldn't locate it. When I finally came upon it the discovery was purely by accident, Pooka stumbling and dislodging a rock that revealed the dark stone. "Stay here," I whispered, sliding off his back. He gave me a disgusted look before I left him and hurried to the entrance. The only problem was the solid wall of rock that showed no way in. I stared at it, remembering how it had opened when I placed my palms there. But this time when I did so, nothing happened. And then it came to me. I was no longer the Willow.

When I returned to Pooka his golden eyes reminded me so much of Gan Ceanach that I began to cry. "At least you still

113

have magic," I murmured, wondering how I could use it to find my lover. "Pooka, take me to Gan Ceanach," I ordered. I had never spoken to him in this tone and wondered what he would do. But once I was on his back he obediently trotted off, turning onto an unfamiliar trail. Was he actually obeying me this time?

Pooka took me deep into another mountain range, his hooves sliding along narrow tracks covered in ice and snow. We were moving along one of these when I noticed blue sky in the distance. I glanced upward at the gray snow-filled clouds before I gazed again at the scene ahead of us. It looked as though a line had been drawn across the landscape, reaching up along the cliffs, across the trail and down into the valley on the other side. On our side was a gray sky and snow, on the other, bright sun shone down on a lush green paradise. A valley lay below, a curving river shining silver in the distance. We moved across the border into a warm and fragrant land where brightly colored birds flew, their calls like the sweet tinkling of many bells. I turned to look back at the gray and dismal world we'd left behind. It was so warm here that I pulled the heavy coat off and draped it in front of me.

Pooka continued on, climbing a steep hill and then following a narrow trail along a ridge that overlooked the green and verdant meadows below. Could this be where the Fae lived? If so I could understand why Gan Ceanach hadn't returned. I would find him now, I was sure of it.

As we rose into misty clouds it became harder to breathe in the thin air. We arrived at a wider trail that leveled out, and not long after that Pooka stopped in front of a wooden door set into the rock face. I smiled and patted my Fae horse. "Thanks, Pooka." I slid off, as excited as a schoolgirl, joy bubbling up at the thought of seeing the faery again. When I approached the opening I was surprised to see pentagrams and moon and star symbols carved into the wood. I had my hand out to knock when the door opened, revealing a youngish woman with brown hair curling around her oval face. Aside from her violet eyes she looked completely ordinary.

"You finally found me," she said, a smile lighting up her otherwise unremarkable features. "Come in, Maeve."

I turned to Pooka who stared at me impassively. "It was Pooka who found you," I responded, following her inside.

"Pooka is one of the Fae," she said agreeably, closing the door behind me.

"Is Gan Ceanach here?"

"No dear. Gan Ceanach is part of the Faery realm. I am a witch. My name is Meg."

"But I distinctly told Pooka to—"

"Pooka will only do your bidding if it is in your best interest, and finding Gan Ceanach does not fit into that category. You are bewitched, Maeve, and without my help you will soon die of this affliction."

"No. That is not true. He loves me, I know it." I turned to leave when I felt her surprisingly strong hand come onto my arm.

"You must remain here with me until I have severed the connection between you and Gan Ceanach. Your horse was wise to bring you to me. I am a witch and a healer and I have had many dealings with the Fae. Not all are evil like Gan Ceanach. Sit here," she ordered, gesturing to a chair next to a rustic table.

A candle burned in a holder, the flame turning blue, then gold, and then violet. My eyelids grew heavy as I stared at the changing colors. "Why are the Fae in Otherworld?"

"They've come back because the realm in which they were living is dying. They have lost their magic and this is why Gan Ceanach has stolen all of yours. His only intention in seducing you was to take your powers and give them to his people."

"Then why didn't he take them the first time he made love to me?"

"Because he needed to gain your trust and your devotion. He was only able to take them because you were already under his spell." Meg moved around the room gathering things from the shelves lining the walls. She placed a pentagram made of some shiny metal in the middle of the table and next to it added a small, stoppered bottle, a sprig of lilac and an ancient coin. "Keep looking at the flame, Maeve, and tell me what you see."

I did as she asked, surprised to see Harold's worried face as he rode along a forest trail on Argyll's back. The scene changed to my baby being breast fed by a woman I didn't recognize, and after that my mother running frantically as though being chased. A second later MacCuill's face loomed up, followed by Duncan's worried eyes, and then my grandfather Eron, who strode through a dark forest as though searching for something.

"The images you see show all the people who love you and are worried about you. Did you see Gan Ceanach among them?"

"No, but that doesn't mean he doesn't love me."

"Can you show me any evidence that will prove his love?"

I looked away from the flame, the spots in my eyes making it hard to focus on her. "He made love to me in the forest. He said he loved me."

"Did he really say those words? Think back. The Fae can prevaricate and deceive, but they do not lie."

I thought about our first time together, trying to recall his words. No, he had never said he loved me, but he had certainly acted as though he did. "But the way he—"

Meg smiled sadly. "Gan Ceanach is very skilled at what he does. Did you know there are several others in Otherworld who are in your same predicament? You were his most important quarry, but that doesn't stop him from seducing other women. He isn't known as the love talker for nothing."

"I don't believe you."

"Drink this," she said, holding out the tiny bottle.

It was unstoppered now and I sniffed but couldn't detect a scent. "What is it?"

"It will help clear your mind."

"But I don't want to clear my mind if it means letting go of—"

"Drink it, Maeve!"

Her voice had lost its sweetness and when I met her implacable gaze I was afraid for a second. I tipped it up and swallowed the thick tasteless liquid, afraid of what she might do next. It hit my stomach with a vengeance and for a moment I thought I might be sick. I was suddenly cold, goose bumps rising on my bare skin.

Meg wrapped a shawl around me before retrieving a small crystal ball from the shelf. She slid her hand over it and muttered some words I didn't understand. "Look and tell me what you see," she said, pushing it toward me. I stared down, the milky surface melting away to show a scene in a forest. Gan Ceanach was with a pale and beautiful young woman, her eyes guileless and enraptured as she stared up at him. And what he was about to do was unmistakable. I turned away and pushed the globe back toward her. "You're a witch, you could have conjured this."

"What would I have to gain by lying, Maeve?"

"He told me that Morrighan has bewitched the ravens and is planning something. He wanted me to align with him to take her down."

"Now, that *is* interesting," Meg said, looking past my right shoulder. "Tell me his exact words."

"I can't remember his exact words!" I answered, exasperated. "He will come for my help, I'm sure of it."

Meg returned her gaze to mine. "Even after taking all your powers?"

I lowered my head as the tears came, and when I felt her place her hand gently on my shoulder I shook it off. "No," I muttered. "He loves me—he has to. I'll die if I don't see him again."

"You'll die whether you see him again or not, Maeve. And that is exactly why Pooka brought you to me. Look at the flame again and don't turn your eyes from it until I tell you to do so."

For some reason I obeyed her, even though my insides were roiling. I felt hollowed out and empty and at the same time sick inside with a feeling I'd never had before. I thought I'd be happy if I just fell to the floor and died. If I didn't have him what was the point of living? But I also wanted to heave up everything I'd ever thought or felt, my stomach churning and on fire.

"Keep looking at the flame," I heard the witch say. I could hear her moving about the room, but when I tried to look away she clapped her hands, reminding me not to. "Study what's there," she said. And when I looked again I saw Harold on a familiar trail, the one Pooka and I had just traveled. I didn't want him here. "Don't let him find me!" I shouted.

Meg was behind me, I could feel her breath on my neck, and then I heard a clang as though a large gong had been rung. My ears reverberated with it. "Don't look away!" she shouted as I swiveled to see what was happening. If she thought I was just going to let her take Gan Ceanach away from me she had another think coming. "No!" I screamed. "I love him—I love him!"

"Do you?" she asked, her voice hoarse and filled with the sound of a crone's venom. "Look again and tell me what you see."

And this time when I looked into the globe Gan Ceanach was there, his handsome face contorting into that of a hideous creature with pockmarked skin and a body bent with age. I could hear him laugh, the same tinkling laugh I'd heard when we were together, but this time his gnarled hands were around a woman's neck, the claws digging in and drawing blood as he squeezed the life out of her. Her eyes bulged as she took her last breath, her face going slack. "No!" I screamed, and then I was falling sideways, blackness mercifully taking me away.

I woke sometime later in a soft bed and covered in an eiderdown quilt. I was shivering all over and thought I might be sick. "Meg," I called weakly, bringing her running from another room. But before I could stop myself I vomited onto the floor, retching on and on until nothing more could come up. And while I did so her hands held my hair back, her fingers cool and soothing on my forehead. When I lay back exhausted she waved her hands, taking away all the mess and stench and leaving the scent of roses behind.

"That is good, Maeve," she assured me, her fingers smoothing the hair back from my forehead. "It is the spell leaving you. You are nearly clear of it."

When I tried to recall the recent past all I could remember was arriving at her door. "What happened?"

"You saw his true form and that gave you the strength to push back from his magic. I couldn't do it for you, Maeve. You had to see it for yourself and realize the truth. Any more time and it would have been too late. His magic grows the longer you carry it inside."

I thought of my baby, my heart contracting with fear. "I left my baby, she—"

"Airmid is fine."

"How do you know?"

Meg smiled and sat on the edge of the bed. "So many people have been calling out to me about you, Maeve. You are very well loved here. I received their messages and knew that eventually you would find your way to me."

"And my powers?"

She shook her head. "They are gone for good unless you can find a way to restore them. I do not know of any."

I took in that news, my eyes welling. "I've hurt Harold so badly. I wouldn't be surprised if he never spoke to me again."

"Shall we test that?" she asked, rising from the bed. "Harold!" she called out.

A second later he was standing in the doorway, his worried hazel eyes on mine.

"Oh my god, Harold." I reached for him, unable to stop the tears. He was by the bed in two strides. He sat and pulled me to him, holding me while I sobbed.

Chapter Sixteen

arold kept Pooka in his sights, following the Fae horse through the deep snow-filled woods. He'd left Maeve knowing that arguing with her would do absolutely nothing. She was convinced of Gan Ceanach's love, her bewitchment complete. The main thing he worried about now was her lack of clothing, her bare legs and feet that were turning blue again and the deep bleeding cuts on her soles. When he'd held her he could feel every one of her ribs. She was slowly wasting away.

When she came to a stop in front of a wall of rock Harold puzzled over her intentions, watching her slide off and head to a spot that looked slightly indented. She screamed and pounded on the stone, finally giving up and telling Pooka in a loud voice to take her to Gan Ceanach. The black horse absorbed that command and then trotted off as though he knew exactly where he was going. Pooka was part of the Fae, but Harold couldn't imagine the creature putting Maeve into more danger.

He followed discreetly, but as the trail narrowed and grew steep he had to stay further and further back. The rocks that Argyll kicked noisily off the cliff would surely alert her that someone was following. It was hours of riding before they entered an entirely different ecosystem, the change coming suddenly as though an invisible wall lay between one side and the other. Here there was no snow, temperatures climbing to levels he hadn't felt since summer. He removed his wool shirt and tied it around his waist, leaving on his homespun tunic.

The trail kept climbing, finally entering misty clouds where the air grew thin. When the wisps parted his jaw dropped in amazement, the view taking what little breath he had away. Emerald green valleys stretched one after the other below him, the sea a dark sapphire in the distance. He stopped for a few moments to stare before moving forward again, hoping he wasn't about to catch up with her. He pulled Argyll to a stop when he heard voices. When he dismounted and crept forward she was standing in front of a doorway that seemed to lead directly into the mountain A normal looking woman with brown curls was talking with her and a moment later Maeve followed her inside. He left Argyll where he was and moved close to the entrance to wait.

It was an hour before the door opened again, this time the woman appearing outside. She looked around and then softly called his name. He stood and came forward.

"There you are," she said pleasantly, steering him inside. She pointed to a chair and then sat across from him. "As you know Maeve is here. I've done what I can for her and now it is up to her."

"Who are you?"

"I'm sorry, didn't I say? I'm Meg, a witch and a healer. I have given her a potion, and if all goes as I hope, Maeve will soon be free of the spell. If she is not, then I fear for her life."

Harold blanched, his hand going involuntarily to the small knife he wore on his belt.

"No need for violence, Harold, at least not against me." She smiled.

"Just a tic of mine, I suppose, since the war."

"Understandable," she acknowledged. "When she wakes I will call you in, but until that time you must remain seated here at this table. Do you understand?"

"I suppose so, although I'm not sure—"

"You don't need to know the why's, Harold, only that there is potent magic here and I am attempting to control it."

He nodded, realizing that he did feel a sort of crackling in the air. It was making the hairs on his arms stand up. A moment later Maeve called out her name, bringing the woman to her feet. She disappeared into the other room, leaving him alone. When he heard the violent retching begin and go on and on, it was all he could do not to rush into the room. But something told him to obey her, and so he kept his feet firmly planted on the floor. He could barely stand to hear her so sick and hoped to the gods that it would be over soon. It was sometime before the door opened again. "Harold?" He turned to see Meg gesturing for him to come in.

He was up in a flash, two strides bringing him to the doorway. Maeve lay against pillows in a soft bed under layers of covers, her face as pale as ash. She looked terribly ill and he wondered how she could possibly be cured. When her gaze met his what he saw there was a mixture of regret and love and some other emotion he couldn't quite identify. It took less than a breath for him to reach her side. And when he sat and pulled her crying into his arms he felt the world lift off his shoulders.

Chapter Seventeen

I couldn't keep my eyes off Harold as Meg talked to both of us about what to expect. His face was so familiar and yet it had been lost to me as I sank deeper and deeper into the faery's spell. He held my hand as Meg talked, squeezing it occasionally. I wore a simple soft brown dress with long sleeves that Meg had given me, with a lace-up bodice that fit me well. My feet were encased in boots supplied to me by Meg as well, but I mourned the loss of my handmade ones and felt angry that Gan Ceanach had chosen to dispose of them so blithely. Another act of many I held against him.

"I will supply you both with food imbued with magic to tide you over," Meg said, looking pointedly at me.

I knew how thin I was, how little I'd eaten in the past weeks.

"Also," she continued, "there may be some relapses in the next few weeks. If you find yourself turning away from Harold or your baby, or any of the people you have always loved, I want you to call out to me. You don't have your magic, but I have mine, and I will hear you and send what energy I can. If Gan Ceanach approaches you ever again you are to say these words, which I will translate into English so that you might remember them: *I call to the north for the power of wind, I call on the south for the power of light, I call on the east for inspiration, I call on the west for strength. These four things will keep me safe from harm.* And do not look him in the eye whatever you do."

"But what if—"

"I doubt very seriously that you will ever see him again. He has gotten what he wanted from you."

Harold frowned, his eyes meeting mine. "What does that mean?"

"It means I'm no longer the Willow, Harold. He took my magic."

"He what? How is that possible? What if you're needed here? I've been hearing rumors ever since you mentioned the ravens."

"Yes, there could be something brewing," Meg said, turning her calm gaze on me. "You are not the only means of stopping evil, Maeve."

"But I was," I said, my voice cracking.

"You will find another way," she said with a surety that I didn't feel. After that she bustled us out the door, handing me an enormous basket. "Do not forget what I told you," she warned.

Harold led the way on Argyll while I trailed behind him, my mind processing everything I'd been through. My body felt drained and insubstantial, as though I'd lost much more than weight. I obviously needed time to recover from my ordeal, but if something was brewing in Otherworld I had to find a way to retrieve my powers. According to Meg there was no way I could. I'd been faced with such dilemmas in the past. It couldn't be insurmountable.

As we moseyed down the hill in the warm sunshine I began to feel better than I had in a long while. I could see Harold's straight back, his narrow hips moving in rhythm with Argyll as the horse negotiated the steep terrain. We were together and heading back to be with our baby. My heart lifted at the thought.

It was only later when I tried to sense anything about Morrighan and the ravens that I realized my mind was as blank as an unpainted canvas. In my obsession with the faery I hadn't noticed the extent of what he'd done to me. Abruptly my mood changed. I felt more vulnerable than I had since my first days in Otherworld, the magic I'd taken for granted sliced neatly away by an entity that I vowed to bring down.

"We are about to enter our realm," Harold called out, pointing toward the wall of gray clouds in the distance. "Shall we spend the night here?"

"I think we should press on. If I get cold I'll wrap up with the heavy cloak Meg gave me."

Harold turned in the saddle. "Are you sure? We could...you know..." He lifted his eyebrows and cocked his head to one side.

"We already did that, Harold," I reminded him, laughing. We had stopped shortly after we left the witch's house to eat, and when we were finished one thing had led to another until we were wrapped in each other's arms, reconnecting with a vigor I didn't know I had.

"I'm not finished with you," he grinned.

"I hope you're never finished with me," I replied. "But right now I'm anxious to see Airy."

We ended up sleeping in the woods close to where I'd been with Gan Ceanach. Harold discovered a cave beneath the cliff edge where the snow couldn't reach us. He'd thought to bring along a warm blanket, and after we'd eaten more of the food, we snuggled under it together, leaving the horses to forage for the lush grass under the layer of snow.

After the last few days of excitement Harold and I both promptly fell asleep. And because of how deeply we slept neither one of us heard the sounds of rustlers who came by during the wee hours to steal our horses and our food.

"Godammit!" I heard Harold shout, waking fully as adrenaline shot through me.

"What's wrong?"

"The horses and our food are gone!" he yelled, staring around wild-eyed.

"Are you sure? Sometimes they wander off."

His dark eyes met mine. "Believe me, Maeve, I know what I'm talking about. There are footprints all over this place. Two men of average size came through here during the night and stole them."

"What are we going to do?"

Harold shook his head, his mouth in a thin line. "We have to walk—what other choice do we have?"

"I bet it was the Fae," I said, pushing myself up to standing. "It's just the sort of thing they like to do."

"Do they come in man-sized bodies?"

"They come in whatever form they choose." It was freezing cold and by the look of things snow would be falling any minute. I sighed heavily and went into the forest. When I pressed my breasts I was surprised to find them nearly empty. I hoped my milk would return; the lack of food and stress had depleted me in many ways.

When I got back Harold was ready to go, his blanket folded and tied on over his warm coat. He handed me my cloak. "I figure we have twenty or more miles of hard trail to get through before nightfall. At least I thought to keep my sword close." He held up the scabbard, the sword handle glowing dully in the gloom.

I followed him to where we'd left the path and then the two of us began what would turn out to be a very long day.

CHAPTER EIGHTEEN

Harold was furious with himself for letting this happen. If he hadn't been so complacent, so sure that everything was on the right track, he would have been alert for trouble. As it was they'd lost two valuable horses, one of which was magic, the other his close companion. And in this weather and terrain they were badly needed. The food was another matter that made him want to scream. All that magic wasted on what—who? The Fae? And Maeve needed it to get her strength back, especially if she planned to resume feeding their baby.

He shook his head, trying to concentrate on the present. Maeve was exhausted and he was sure that at some point he would need to carry her. And if he were honest with himself, he was beyond tired as well. His frantic ride to Duncan's and then the trip through snow and ice had drained him more than he cared to admit, not to mention following her all the way to the witch's house. This was going to be a very long day.

"What are you thinking?" he heard Maeve ask.

He shook his head dismissively, not wanting to worry her. "Not much. Just wondering how far it is to Tiadan."

"If you're worried about me, I'm fine," she said, her mouth curling up in a smile. "I'm energized at the thought of Airy."

"Glad to hear it. I'll keep that in mind when you fall down and I have to carry you."

She made a moue and then laughed. "All will be well."

"Since you don't have your magic I know that isn't a premonition, but where is it coming—?" His voice trailed off as he saw her face drop, her expression turning to one of despair. He took hold of her arm, turning her to face him. "God, I'm sorry, Maeve. I wasn't thinking when I said that."

She pulled away. "It's fine. It just takes some getting used to."

Harold didn't know what to say so he didn't say anything, his concentration going to where he put his feet. The trail was treacherous, hiding pointed rocks and broken off sticks that dug into the soles of his boots. When tiny flakes began to fall he had to laugh. "They say the small ones are the worst," he said, looking up.

"The small snowflakes accumulate faster and seem to stick," she agreed, pushing ahead of him down a narrow hill.

"Be careful," he called, following at a slower pace. But when she tripped and tumbled down he ran after her. He pulled her to her feet, brushing the snow off her cloak. "Are you okay?" Her wince of pain answered that question.

"I did something to my ankle."

"And no healing powers either," he muttered to himself.

"I heard that, Harold. I'm sorry I can't be more use to you," she said in a hurt tone.

"Jesus Christ, Maeve! I was only commenting. You have to admit that having healing abilities would help right now." He lifted her into his arms and continued on, trying not to think about how tired his muscles were or how his legs buckled when he tried to climb the steep hill looming in front of him.

But the worst came an hour later when the wind began to howl, the temperature dipping lower and lower. As the storm grew in intensity Harold finally had to stop. When he placed Maeve on the ground the snow came at them so hard it knocked her off her feet and flung her against a tree. Harold managed to keep standing, but only barely until the next blast took him down. He crawled to where Maeve lay with her head to one side with her eyes closed. "Holy shit," he said, staring at the spread of bright red against the snow. He carefully examined the split in her scalp, determining that it wasn't deep. But she still hadn't opened her eyes. Another blast of wind came up, flinging branches around, limbs cracking and slamming down with more force than seemed possible. His arms were left cut and bleeding, and if he hadn't ducked in time, an enormous branch would have landed directly on his head. This was no ordinary storm.

He dragged Maeve to a small dip in the uneven terrain, trying to get out of the wind. "Wake up," he said softly, giving her cheek a slap. But she didn't, and after a while he began to worry. Something strange was going on, the storm moving around as though searching them out. He pulled Maeve to sitting and tried to wake her, his fingers going to her neck to check her pulse. He'd almost lost her once in the past week, was this to be the day she died? But her pulse was steady.

He sat with his back against ledge rock, holding her close as the wind whipped and whined around him like a rabid animal trying to get at its prey. And then he remembered the words Meg had taught Maeve to ward off Gan Ceanach. He said them out loud, his voice growing stronger with each sentence: *I call to the north for the power of wind, I call on the south for the power of light, I call on the east for inspiration, I call on the west for strength. These four things will keep me safe from harm.* His voice rang out, and when he was finished the wind stopped as abruptly as it started.

A second later Maeve opened her eyes. "What happened?"

Harold shook his head, trying to smile. "The Fae nearly killed us."

Maeve looked around. "The Fae? All I remember is wind."

"That's because you were unconscious. I'm telling you they conjured this storm. I'm sure they're the ones who have Pooka and Argyll."

She stared at him skeptically. "I think your imagination is getting the better of you."

Harold frowned. "Give me some credit here, Maeve. Just because you have to rely on me now doesn't mean you get to downplay everything I say. I know what I just experienced and that was no ordinary wind. I stopped it with the words Meg taught you."

"Really? You remembered them?"

Harold shook his head, irritated. "Shall we move on now?" This day was going from bad to worse, he thought, picking her up to trudge back to where they'd left the path.

It was growing dark by the time Harold called it a day. "I'm exhausted and I would imagine you are too." He placed her carefully down. "How does your ankle feel?"

"A little better but I still can't put weight on it. How much further do you think we have to go?"

"I'd say at least ten miles, although I'm not exactly sure where we are. Do you recognize these woods?"

"Are you telling me we're lost?" Maeve asked, her voice shrill.

Harold grinned sheepishly. "Maybe. I've tried to head northwest figuring that eventually we'd come to the sea."

Maeve scoffed and sat down to remove her boot. "How can you tell direction with such a thick cloud cover?" She bent to her foot. "It's really bruised and swollen," she said, looking up.

Harold examined her ankle, surprised to see how bad it looked. "If only we had some arnica," he muttered.

"It grows around here somewhere but probably not at this time of year."

"And it would be impossible to find in the dark," he added, leaning back against a tree and closing his eyes.

"Are you planning to feed us or are we going to starve out here?"

Harold opened his eyes and stared at her. "You expect me to go hunting in the snow and storm and then make a fire and skin and cook whatever I catch?"

Maeve shrugged. "When you put it that way it does sound kind of extreme."

"Yeah, Maeve—it is extreme and I don't have the energy right now." He closed his eyes again, feeling her snuggle into him. He put his arm around her and pulled her close. "Try and get some rest."

But the day was not over.

CHAPTER NINETEEN

"Harold, did you hear that?" I sat up, trying to see into the shadows.

Harold groaned. "This better be important. I was dreaming I was warm and eating stew and homemade bread."

"Something woke me up," I whispered. "Can you check?"

"So now you want me to scout around in the dark for monsters?"

"I'm serious. Whatever woke me is still out there."

Harold let out a long sigh and rose to his feet. I watched him head away under the trees, hoping I was wrong. A second later I heard a whoosh like the flapping of large wings and then his piercing scream. "Harold!" I shouted, trying to hobble after him. But my foot wouldn't hold me and I went down, falling heavily on my hip.

A second later Harold burst from under the canopy. "There are hundreds of birds or something in there. They dive-bombed me!"

I saw blood trickling down his cheek, bleeding cuts on his hands. "What do we do?" I asked stupidly.

My question was lost as a flock of something big and dark flew at us. I held my hands over my head while Harold tried to fight them, his sword out in a flash. I watched him slashing at the strange creatures, heard the horrible grating screams they made when he cut them down. It seemed like hours of this before the rest of them flew off, the flap of their wings diminishing as they disappeared into the dark. "What are they?" I crawled over to where Harold lay on the ground breathing hard.

"I don't know, but there's couple of dead ones over by that tree."

I crawled to where he pointed but it was too dark to make anything out. "Can't see," I whispered.

Harold rose and came to get me, half carrying me back to where we'd been sleeping. "At least they're dead," he said. "Now we have to hope the rest of them don't attack again." He placed his sword on the ground and put an arm around my shoulders, settling back into our shelter. He closed his eyes. "We can examine them in a couple of hours."

"How can you be so calm?"

"I'm too tired to be anything else," he muttered. And a second later he was snoring.

I lay awake thinking about the ravens that attacked us in Tiadan. Could what Gan Canach said about Morrighan be true? But even without my magic I had the strong feeling that Morrighan was not involved in whatever was going on here. No. This had to be the Fae. I was no longer a threat to them and Harold had never had magic to begin with, aside from being the reincarnated first king of Scotland. So why were they attacking us?

I dozed for a while and when I woke again the sky had lightened. The clouds had lifted away and it looked like it could be sunny if another storm didn't blow in. Harold was crouched by whatever he'd killed the night before. I tried to stand and let out a sharp cry of pain and crumpled to the ground.

He turned. "Stay there. I'll come get you." A moment later his arm was around my waist. "Put your arm around my neck—you have to see this."

He let me use him as a crutch, supporting me the fifteen or twenty feet to where they lay. I looked down on two ashen-faced, somewhat human-looking creatures with jet-black, lank, and filthy hair. They stunk of decay. Their fingers ended in long claws and black feathery wings protruded from their backs. Blood had pooled around them from the lethal cuts Harold had inflicted with his sword. "They look somewhat like the men I saw at Samhain."

"Was your lover among them?"

I gave him a look, annoyed by the sarcastic tone. "Don't call him *your lover*, Harold. I couldn't help it. And yes, I think he was, but he doesn't resemble these creatures. I never saw wings on his back and he didn't have claws."

Harold picked up a bit of clothing here, an arm there, trying to get an idea of what they were. "I've never encountered anything like this," he finally said.

"Nor I. But I'm sure they're Fae."

"Why do you say that?"

"Look at them, Harold. They are obviously changelings—they're human-like but they fly, and they stink like rot."

"And those are attributes of the Fae?"

"There are so many different species of Fae; it's like comparing ants to cockroaches." I stared at them again, the increasing stench bringing bile up my throat. "Let's get out of here before I'm sick."

Harold stood and strapped on his sword. "Shall I carry you again or do you want to try and walk?"

"Carry, please," I asked, lifting my arms like a helpless child. Not only didn't I have magic, but also couldn't even walk on my own. What a weakling I'd turned into.

Harold grunted as he lifted me, his face contorting.

"Am I so heavy?"

"My legs are sore from yesterday and my muscles feel like mush. I wish we had the horses."

Just as he said that I heard a nicker and Pooka trotted out from under the trees. Behind him the piebald lumbered into view. Both horses had been stripped of saddles and bridles. "Apparently your wish has been granted." Harold helped me up on Pooka's bare back and then to my surprise did a vaulting leap, landing squarely on Argyll. "Still have your Kenneth skills, I see."

He grinned. "Comes in handy at times like these. Who do you think took them? It couldn't have been those creatures."

"Why not? They certainly look capable of riding astride, and besides, from what I've read, nearly all Fae can change shape at will."

"They didn't take our horses in order to ride, Maeve. They took them to put us in danger, which worked very well."

"And yet here we are," I said gaily, pressing Pooka forward with my thighs. The sun was streaming through the bare branches now, sending shafts of light shimmering across the snow and making it glitter. Despite feeling that we were being hunted I felt happy to be alive.

It was probably around two hours later that we came upon Dougal, his eyes widening in surprise when he saw us. .

"Ye found her!" he cried out, running toward us. "Maeve's here!" he shouted, cupping his hands around his mouth. "We've been searching since ye left, Harold."

"I wish I could have let you know, but—"

"Don't bother explainin'. There's plenty of time for catchin' up. I'll gather the group and ye can travel with us to Caer Sidi."

"We're heading to Tiadan," I said, glancing at Harold. "Our baby's there."

"Not anymore." Dougal smiled. "Tannith brought her down a day and a half ago, said she'd had some psychic hunch about where you two would end up."

Harold frowned "Wasn't it your wife who was taking care of Airy?"

"Aye, she was. Now your bairn is with Rea."

I thought about Rea, realizing how glad I would be to see her. Airy had been well taken care of in my absence, but still I felt an enormous guilt for having left her without even a backward glance. My hand went involuntarily to my chest, worried that I had nothing to feed her.

The trip from where we were to Caer Sidi was not long, all of us laughing and talking as we traveled together. Harold insisted that MacCuill ride Argyll. "I need to stretch my legs," I heard him tell the druid. But I knew it was because of how tired MacCuill looked, as though the cares of the world had come down on his shoulders. Something wasn't right. But despite all that my good mood persisted. If there were a problem we would solve it as we always had. In my enthusiasm I had forgotten completely that I no longer had magic.

As soon as Harold and I rode up to Rea's small house, she appeared in her doorway, her perceptive gaze assessing me. "Are you all right?"

I nodded and smiled, slanting a glance at Harold before slipping off Pooka's bare back. I hobbled toward her and reached out to hug her. "The witch got rid of the spell."

"Witch? How did you find her?"

"Pooka found her. I was searching for Gan Ceanach."

Rea let out a relieved sigh. "I'm sure you'd like to see Airy; she has been a delight and I will miss her, although having two to deal with has certainly cut into my sleep." She laughed.

I couldn't stop the tears when I saw my baby in the willow crib next to Rea's baby boy. Her cheeks were pink with health, her bright eyes taking everything in. When I picked her up she snuggled into me, the feel of her warm body against mine such a comfort.

I was undoing the laces of my dress when Rea put her small hand on my arm. "I fed her not long ago."

I felt disappointment and resentment, the need to feed her overwhelming me for a second before I got control of myself. "Thanks for taking such good care of her," I managed.

When Harold took her out of my arms and held her up in the air she let out a sound I had never heard her make, somewhere between a chortle and a real laugh.

"Tea?" Rea asked, retrieving three small earthenware cups.

"I have heard of the creatures you describe," Rea said, answering Harold's questions about what had attacked us. "They are known as the Sluagh, a species of Fae who fly in flocks at night and collect souls."

I let out a little gasp. "You mean souls of the dead or the living?"

Rea raised one shoulder. "Either one, I hear. You are very lucky you had Harold with you."

A feeling of irritation went through me. I was not used to relying on Harold to keep me safe. "Why are they here, Rea? Is it about me?" I turned to Harold. "Us?"

"MacCuill seems to think it's the beginning of a larger conflict between two factions of Fae. As far as Gan Ceanach and this latest incident, it certainly looks like you were targeted. What did the witch say?"

"She only acknowledged that something might be brewing."

"That is an understatement. It has not happened here in Caer Sidi, but I heard rumors that the Sluagh attacked a village to the south and several villagers were killed."

I stared at her. "Why didn't you say?"

Rea sighed. "I just did say, Maeve. I cannot blurt out every detail of everything I know in a minute."

"I'm sorry, Rea. I just feel so vulnerable without my usual ability to see what's coming."

"You had better speak to MacCuill about all that. Perhaps he will have a solution."

"I will, but according to Meg, there is nothing to be done."

While we finished our tea, Rea gathered a few herbs together, soaked them, and treated my ankle. She cupped her hands around the swelling and hummed and purred, the vibration entering the soft tissue and drawing out the inflammation.

"That should help," Rea murmured a few minutes later. "It will be tender to the touch, but I think you will be able to put weight on it now."

The swelling was gone, a lot of the bruising as well. "It feels so much better," I told her, moving it around in a circle. "Thank you."

When Rea's baby woke and began to fuss Harold and I took the opportunity to leave. I gave Rea a hug and thanked her for everything, glad that I was again able to feel love and gratitude toward my friends.

"Does Rea have a husband?" Harold asked when we got out of earshot.

I laughed. " I know the baby has a father but I've never met him. For all I know they couple with whomever they deem is right at the time."

"Selective breeding as nature intended. Not a bad way to go. It would certainly cut down on boredom."

I gave him a look. "Are you saying--?"

Harold let out a laugh that rang through the still air. "Are you kidding? I don't have time to be bored around you; who knows what crazy antics you'll be up to next?"

CHAPTER TWENTY

Harold kept a close eye on Maeve for signs of relapse, not entirely trusting that she was spell free. Their visit to pick up Airy had gone well and now they were ensconced in Duncan's unusual dwelling and Maeve had taken the opportunity to feed the baby. He could see by her rapt expression the pleasure it gave her and had a moment of envy wishing men could do the same.

"So, Harold, what is yer plan?" he heard Duncan ask.

He turned to the older man. "Ask the boss."

"I am no longer the boss," Maeve answered, her eyes meeting his.

In her look he saw the sadness this statement produced, as well as her irritation at having to rely on anyone else. "So maybe the first order of business is getting your powers back?"

She shook her head and bent to the baby who had fallen asleep. He watched her pull her dress up and tighten the laces. "How would we do that?" she finally asked. "No. I think the first order of business is to find out what's going on. Are the Fae attacking Otherworld or are they fighting amongst themselves?"

"Aye. That is a good question," Duncan acknowledged. "As I mentioned the last time I saw ye, Queen Druantia may have some answers for ye."

Maeve's eyes clouded. "I—"

When an expression of indecision and then fear appeared on her face, Harold took over. "To have an audience with the queen means seeking out MacCuill again. The druid looked ill on the trip back."

"MacCuill is dealin' with a lot right now. The queen has been failin' for a while and may not last long. But I'm sure he will welcome ye and do what he can to help."

"I wish we'd thought to ask him all this on our trip here," Maeve said quietly. "I hate to burden him when he already has so much on his plate."

"Dinna worry yourself, Maeve. This Fae problem is on everyone's shoulders. Even the queen, in her diminished state, will be discussin' it with her advisors."

"Do you have a rucksack or carry pack we could use?" Harold asked, pointing to the baby.

Duncan looked confused for a moment before his eyes brightened. "I have just the thing," he said, moving toward a shelf.

Before they headed off to locate the horses Harold stopped and took hold of Maeve's arm. "Talking to MacCuill may kill two birds with one stone. He must know how to get your magic back."

Maeve gazed at him bleakly. "I think if he did he would have mentioned it while we were traveling. I would rather accept it than get my hopes up. Meg very clearly stated that there was no way."

"There is always a way—how did you get your magic to begin with?"

Maeve shrugged. "The moonstone at first, then the werewolf root the healing goddess gave me, and then—I don't know. It just seemed that one day I could move through the ether just by thinking where I wanted to go, and I could heal with my hands."

Harold frowned, grabbing Argyll's long tangled mane as they came close to where the horses grazed. "It was happening before you left home, Maeve. Remember your encounter in Milltown with the ravens? And what about your premonitions, the vision of me wearing a crown?"

"I was taking peyote at the time, Harold."

He turned to stare at her, remembering back to their camping trip, the visions they both had—the strength Maeve exuded. "It was more than that. Whatever you had is part of you and can't be removed by one bad member of the Fae."

"I beg to differ. I feel different—kind of hollow and washed out."

"Maybe it's because the baby just drained you. You've hardly eaten in days. I'm surprised you had any milk to give her."

She looked at him bleakly. "I didn't. The only reason she was satisfied is because Rea fed her not long ago."

They reached the horses and Harold gave her a leg up onto Pooka's back. Once she was settled he handed her up the pack they'd reconfigured into a papoose. Her moods seemed to shift like the wind, one minute up, the next minute down. She wasn't herself. "Let's go and talk with MacCuill. At least we'll get a better idea what we're up against."

Maeve shrugged. "Whatever you think is best."

They had crossed the river and were heading along the eastern edge of the forest when Maeve suddenly said, "Maybe I'm dying."

"What?"

"I don't feel right, Harold. My body is weak and there's something—a sensation that I'm emptying out. If it all goes, I'll be dead."

Harold looked over at her, noticing the pallor in her normally rosy skin. She'd been ashen for a while but this reached a new level. Her eyes looked sunken when earlier they'd been bright. "This sounds surprisingly like a premonition, Maeve. Tell me more." He held her gaze trying as hard as he could to send her a message. Would she pick it up?

"Yes, I know you love me," she said, her gaze sliding away, "but—"

"You heard me!" he cried out, moving his weight back to bring Argyll to a stop.

Maeve frowned. "What in the world are you talking about?"

"I sent you a telepathic message and you heard it."

"I know how you feel about me—that doesn't prove anything."

"Yes, it does! Don't you see? You just responded to what I said *in your mind*!"

Maeve stopped and turned to him. "I did, didn't I? Maybe there's hope?"

She looked so vulnerable and despairing he wanted to take her in his arms, but they were on horseback, about to head across the snowy meadows that led toward the wide shore and Druantia's castle. "There is definitely hope, Maeve," he said strongly. "Don't give up."

It was dark by the time they reached Queen Druantia's red stone structure at the western end of the shell-shaped cove. The imposing building stood on a high bluff overlooking the sea that at this time of day resembled a solid mass of darkness spreading into infinity. Harold shivered. They followed the wide track that wound around the hill until they were nearly to the top. "Should we leave the horses here?" Harold asked.

"I don't know. Do they have stables or should we just turn them loose?"

"Since no one's discovered us yet let's turn them loose and go and knock." As soon as he said these words two druid guards approached, grey hoods pulled down over their faces.

"What is your business here?" one of them called out in Gaelic. Harold answered in the same language, the ancient words coming from the Kenneth part of him.

They both bowed and waited until Harold and Maeve were on the ground. Once the horses had been turned loose the guards led the way up the hill.

"What did you say?" Maeve whispered.

"I told them who we are and that we've come to see MacCuill."

Maeve let out a sigh. "By their behavior you must have impressed them. I'm glad we don't have to face the queen tonight."

"Who said we don't?"

Once they were inside and MacCuill had been sent for, Airy woke up, her hungry screams echoing off the rough stone walls. "I hope Druantia likes babies," Maeve muttered, removing her cloak and loosening the laces of her dress.

When MacCuill arrived his indigo eyes were drooping with fatigue. "I'm glad you came. I thought to invite you, but in your rush to see Airy I let it go."

Harold glanced at Maeve. "Maeve is not well. She feels—"

"I feel like I'm dying," Maeve finished. "The witch helped me, but now I have the sense that I'm fading away."

"And so you are. Your magic is part of you, an essential piece that if removed is like taking away an organ that you can't do without."

Harold waited for Maeve to respond, but her eyes were downcast watching the baby. "Is there anything we can do?" he finally asked.

MacCuill sighed heavily. "There is more at stake than Maeve's magic, Harold. I've heard that two factions of Faery are warring. Unfortunately the fighting is over Otherworld and which one will take up residence here."

"The Sluagh attacked us," Maeve said without looking up. "Harold killed a couple of them." She moved the baby to the other breast.

"I'm glad you were able to kill them, Harold, but the news of their existence is disturbing. If I didn't have so much going on here I would have paid closer attention. The queen has recently died and the conclave is now in process of picking a new leader."

Maeve's head jerked up. "The queen is dead? I am so sorry, MacCuill."

"We all knew it was coming but still it's been a shock. The brotherhood has lost its center and there's been dissension and chaos the likes of which we've never had before. Druantia was stronger than any of us realized and held us together with an iron hand."

There was a long silence punctuated by the sound of waves crashing on shore. Finally MacCuill leaned toward Maeve. "What you must do is find the Fae who are not in league with Gan Ceanach. They are the only ones who might have the magic to reverse what's been done to you."

"Where do they live?" Harold asked.

"When they were in Otherworld years ago they lived high in the Gualan Mountains. The air is thinner there and it suits them."

"We were in the far western mountains with Meg, the healer. Do they live in that area?" Maeve asked.

"Use your map," MacCuill said.

Harold shook his head. "The map is gone—taken by the faery, if I'm not mistaken."

Maeve nodded. "Among other things."

Harold thought back ten months to the early days of the war. Maeve had been a warrior woman who managed to gather followers from every corner of Otherworld. She healed them, fed them and kept them from losing hope. And now she looked depleted and hopeless, her eyes like those of a lost child. He wasn't sure why this had come on so quickly, but he had to help her even if it meant traversing every corner of Otherworld.

Chapter Twenty-One

Remorse and guilt crept further into my psyche; it dampened my life force and made me want to kill myself. Was this Gan Ceanach's final curse? I had given myself over to the faery, allowing him to not only take my body but also to take what made me *me*. I felt bone tired. The only thing keeping me on the earth was Airy. As long as I could feed her and hold her I was alive. And yet even that seemed in danger of disappearing. I barely had enough milk to sustain her and if I didn't begin to build my own strength she would soon need a supplement.

MacCuill took us to the dining hall, and after we'd eaten he found a room where we could spend the night. "If you are to save her you need to leave early in the morning," I heard him whisper to Harold just before he closed the door.

Harold lit the oil lamp and put his arms around me. "Concentrate on Airy and me. We both love you."

I pulled away, my arms going protectively around my body. "But I don't love myself, Harold. I don't understand what's going on, but I feel like I'm disappearing."

Harold peered at me. "You look solid enough to me."

"Metaphysically speaking," I clarified.

"We'll find the Fae."

"If we find them how do we know if it's the good Fae or the bad Fae?"

Harold grimaced. "It'll be obvious."

"And in the meantime if it's the ones who attacked us we could be killed."

"Do you have another suggestion?"

I shook my head. I climbed into the small bed and pulled Airy close, turning my back on Harold and the world.

It was nearing noon the next day before we reached the mountain pass that led toward the witch's house. We'd come out of the cold and shed our cloaks and coats, the sun warming our stiff limbs as the slanted light turned our shadows into odd shapes. "Shall we veer off on another trail or head up the same way?" I asked.

Harold stared at me, but I knew he didn't see me. He finally said, "Why don't we ask Pooka?"

I brightened immediately, having forgotten that my horse was Fae. I bent to his ear. "Take us to the good Fae, the ones like you," I whispered.

My horse immediately turned around and headed up a steep cliff on an animal track I hadn't noticed. The narrow trail meandered around boulders and ledges, disappearing, only to reappear a few feet up. I leaned forward and held onto his mane to keep from falling off, afraid to look back to see how Argyll and Harold were managing.

It was a long upward climb before we arrived at a flat area where the horses could walk easily. I turned to Harold, noticing the strain on his face.

"I didn't think the big guy could do it," he said, patting Argyll's sweat-covered neck.

Pooka was also sweaty, but I had been hearing Argyll's labored breathing for a while and knew how hard the climb had been for him. I let out a sigh, wondering if there was another climb in our future. The air was thin here and I already felt dizzy from lack of oxygen.

By now the sun was low in the sky and I wondered how much further we had to go. I got my answer a few minutes later when Pooka came to a stop in front of an exquisitely carved doorway set into the stone. Similar to the witch's house it looked as though it led directly into the mountain. We were at least two thousand feet higher than Meg's house and my lungs burned as I tried to suck in air. "Shall I see if they're at home?" But just as I said that the baby began to fuss, woken by the sudden lack of movement. Before I could slide off and take off the pack her cries were echoing through the canyon, scaring a flock of birds that were settling into a scraggly tree for the night.

I had her in my arms and was opening my dress when I heard a hoarse voice ask, "What do you want?"

Out of the corner of my eye I saw Harold jump off Argyll, his sword in his hand.

"Achhh!"

I turned to the grating sound, not surprised to see an ugly hag around five feet tall staring at the last rays of sun glinting off Harold's sword. Her gray hair hung in loose tendrils around an off-balance face and a large bulbous nose, her eyes small and sunken. She held up one gnarled hand and backed away.

To my surprise Harold replaced his sword in the scabbard and stepped toward her. "It's all right. We are not here to harm you. We have come to seek your help."

I held my breath, wondering why Pooka would stop here. These couldn't be the good Fae; this creature was hideously ugly. I'd imagined blonde hair and even features, well-formed ears that came to points. Or was that elves?

"Who are you?" she asked in a voice that grated like two rocks scraping against each other.

"I am Harold/Kenneth of war fame, and this is Maeve, also known as the Willow. Her powers have been taken by Gan Ceanach and now she withers and dies."

The hag turned her ugly face to me, piggy eyes assessing. "We do not like Gan Ceanach or his kind," she croaked. "We are gathering forces to go against them in their lust for new land and new conquests."

I wanted to hold my hands over my ears, but I knew it would offend her. "Can you help me?"

She stared at me for another moment and then turned to Harold. "Leave your magical beast and come inside," she said.

"But—what about—?" I met Harold's gaze, the slight movement of his head telling me not to question anything. And all this time my baby had been stunned into silence, her eyes wide as she watched the proceedings.

"I was only going to ask about Argyll," I whispered as we followed the hag through the very small doorway.

Harold put his finger to his lips, ducking as he headed inside.

Once the door closed—on its own—behind us, I was stunned into a silence of my own. A million tiny lights brought the high-ceilinged room into view. It was a place meant for a goddess, I thought to myself, wondering how people this ugly could have a place so beautiful. The yellow stone glowed with light cast from skylights far above us. Niches filled with lithe figurines of humanoids with wings and others with pointed ears, crowded the walls. Crystals were embedded into the stone, casting prisms when the little moving fairy lights, for lack of a better word, glanced off them. Harold had to grab my hand to pull me away, pointing to our 'host' who was heading through another low doorway.

On the other side of the door was another room, this one furnished in deep red velvet chairs, a long trestle table with benches on either side, and several nooks built into the walls with shelves that housed books and more statuary. I glanced at Harold but he only shook his head, his focus on our tour guide who was now opening yet another door. She turned to us before she entered.

"Do not speak unless spoken to," she cautioned in her raspy voice. "I will announce you." I heard her speak our names before she backed away.

Harold went ahead and I followed, afraid of what it was we were not supposed to speak to. But of course any idea I had in my mind was immediately dashed when we came through the doorway. Sitting in a throne-type chair was the most beautiful woman I'd ever seen, her porcelain skin and luminous eyes contrasting with the halo of spun-gold hair around her shoulders.

"You are the Willow," she said in a mellifluous tone, a smile curling up her full mouth.

"I was," I corrected, returning her smile. "Now I am Maeve, the nothing."

She laughed at the joke I'd made, leaning forward. "Come close, Maeve, the nothing, and let me see the baby."

I moved closer and when she held out her milk-white arms I placed Airy in them. "Oh, what a delight!" she said, holding Airy up to take a look at her. "I would like to have her—would you be willing to trade?"

I stared at her, unable to speak until Harold came up behind me and gave me a nudge. "I—I hope you're joking," I finally managed.

The miracle of beauty looked down at me, her arched eyebrows pulling together. "I do not make jokes," she said.

"I can't give up my baby. She's all I have."

The queen, or whoever she was, glanced at Harold, her eyebrows rising. "You have this man who loves you. Why do you need a baby? You can have another."

"But Airy is my baby—she loves me—I love her. She's part of our family."

"And yet you talk of being nothing. How can you be nothing when you have these things?"

I was beginning to wonder if this was some sort of psychological test. "I—my powers made me who I am," I finally said. "They made me whole. Now I feel empty and scared and vulnerable."

She laughed. "Like all humans, you mean?"

"I suppose that's true." When she held the baby out I took her back, cradling her against my body.

"You will have to convince me why I should care about your magic, Maeve. It seems to me that you have more than most people. I would like to have this man who stands behind you. He could give me a child who would be at least half Fae. I am the queen and the last of the royal line of elves and have no offspring to take over when I die. That of course will be hundreds of years from now, but it is lonely to be the last of one's race."

I turned to Harold, a thought entering my mind. "What would you say if I lent him to you?" I asked, turning back to her.

Harold's hand came onto my arm. "What are you suggesting?" he hissed.

"You had to endure me in love with Gan Ceanach, now you get to spend a night with this gorgeous faery," I whispered.

"I hope this isn't just an illusion for our benefit," he whispered. "If she—"

"I assure you I am exactly as I appear," the queen said. "And in answer to your question, I will agree, on the stipulation that he gives me a child."

"But how will we--?"

"I will know," she said, rising gracefully. "Now, Harold, if you will please follow me?"

I watched the two of them leave by a small door in the wall behind the dais, my mind reeling as I realized what I'd done. Imagining the two of them together nearly made me physically ill; what if he fell in love with her? But my thoughts were cut short when my baby finally realized how hungry she was, her wail bouncing off the stone as she let me know. I was just about to settle into the throne to feed her when our original host came to get me. "Follow me," she ordered, leading into the other room. She pointed toward a common wooden chair and disappeared through another side door.

Chapter Twenty-two

h arold was stunned. He couldn't believe that Maeve would give him over to another woman this easily. She must really want her magic back, he mused, shaking his head.

"I am Aine," the queen said, taking his hand. "I hope you can let go of trepidation and enjoy yourself. It is that which will allow me to conceive. Remember, if we do not make a baby tonight you will need to be with me again."

He met her gaze. She was certainly beautiful with her slim figure, high breasts and skin that looked almost translucent. And there was a hint of kindness marked by the tiny smile lines next to her eyes. But how could Maeve do this? He would never have offered her up like a piece of cake to a complete stranger. Anger was right at the surface but he pushed it down. Maeve was desperate to get her powers back—if this is what it took then so be it.

He followed Aine into a sumptuous bedroom with a canopied four-poster bed hung all around with gossamer white fabric. The curtains blew lazily in a light breeze coming from somewhere he couldn't determine.

"Would you like to bathe first?" she asked.

"Bathe—you have a bathroom here?"

She smiled and led him into a large stone room, a tub set deep into the tiled floor. A silver spigot attached to nothing hung over the tub and when the queen waved a hand over it water burst from the spout, steam rising as it splashed into the tub. "I can join you if you like."

He turned. "I—"

"It would help, I think," she continued. "You seem nervous."

If only you knew how nervous, he thought. It would be a miracle if he could—but now she was undressing, and as he watched her take each article of clothing off he became aroused. Her body was perfect, her breasts round and firm, with nipples the color of pale roses, her belly smooth and flat, the patch of blonde hair between her legs, downy and soft. He quickly removed his pants and shirt, keeping a close eye on her.

When she stepped into the tub he followed, moving to the side opposite of where she'd seated herself.

"It is all right, Harold. I do not bite. If you would wash my back I would be most appreciative." She pointed to a natural sponge and bar of soap that smelled of roses lying on a small table behind the tub.

He picked up the sponge and dipped it into the water before rubbing it over the soap. When he moved closer she turned and held up her hair, pinning it with an invisible clip. Her ears were like perfect shells, the tips slightly pointed. When he touched her back with the sponge she let out a long sigh.

"Do you have any idea how long it's been since I've been touched?"

He didn't answer her as he moved the sponge along her shoulders and down her spine. For some reason he felt sorry for her all alone and one of the last of her race. Everyone needed love, even a faery queen. When she turned to face him, he dropped the sponge, his gaze taken by the droplets of water clinging to her perfect naked body. God, he thought—she is magnificent.

She reached out with both hands and took hold of his face, pulling him to her. And when his lips met hers he was lost for a second, wondering if this was some kind of crazy dream. At this moment he was ready to be her love slave. And when she pulled away and stood he watched the drops of silver pour from her, tiny rainbows reflecting in each one. "It is time," she said, stepping out to retrieve a towel that had materialized in mid air.

He followed her, taking the towel she held out.

"I will wait in the next room."

He dried himself, feeling like a cheating husband, and yet it was Maeve who had set this up. Why not just relax and enjoy it?

In the next room the queen had pushed back the bed curtains and draped herself across the bedclothes. He didn't fail to notice how she'd placed herself to give him the most alluring view. She held out her arms and he moved into them, putting Maeve out of his mind as he did exactly what the queen wanted.

Afterwards they both slept, and when she woke him in the middle of the night, asking him to perform the act one more time just to be sure, he did as she bade him.

Chapter
Twenty-Three

Spriggan, as I'd begun to think of her, showed me into a small room with a narrow bed. Reserved for unimportant guests, I thought to myself. At least it was clean with a window where I could view the new moon coming up. I had been fed a dinner of some kind of stew and given a tankard of ale to wash it down. Now I was tired and worried in equal measure, afraid of what I'd done.

What man could resist a magical faery who looked like that? It was as bad as Gan Ceanach, I thought, wishing I'd never suggested it. Would she just bewitch him and keep him for herself? It was entirely possible from what I knew of the Fae. I fed Airy, surprised that she seemed contented with what she got, and then fell asleep with her in my arms, my dreams taking me places I didn't want to go.

⟨⟩

"Well, what happened?" I asked Harold the next morning when I met him in the dining hall. The baby was already in her pack on my back, quiet for once.

His eyes narrowed before he turned away, busy with buttering his bread and drinking whatever they'd given him.

"Spriggan was kind enough last night," I began. "I slept—"

He turned frowning. "Spriggan? Is that her name?"

"No. It's just the name I—"

"Spriggan is a grotesquely ugly creature from Cornish folklore."

"I know, Harold. I guess that's why the name came to me."

"Unkind, Maeve, and not like you. Her name is Helig. What's going on?"

I stared at him. "For starters the man I love just spent the night with the most beautiful faery I've ever seen."

"And whose idea was that?"

I shook my head and turned to my breakfast, trying to push down the rising nausea. "Are you planning to tell me about it?"

"Why should I? It will only upset you. What I want to know is if you have your magic back—wasn't that a condition of what I did last night?"

"So far I haven't noticed any change. But didn't she say she has to be pregnant? I hope this doesn't mean I'll have to wait until the baby is born." All of a sudden I realized the implications of what I'd arranged. "Harold, you'll be the father of her baby!" I cried out, horrified.

"And this didn't occur to you yesterday when you were bargaining me away?"

"What did she say about it?"

"We didn't do much talking, and what we did talk about was mostly her race and what happened to them."

I noticed how tired he looked, the red rims and shadows under his eyes. "I can tell you didn't sleep much," I muttered.

He grabbed my arm none too gently. "This was all your idea, Maeve. And if I hear one more word of complaint out of your mouth I'll be riding down this mountain alone."

I pulled out of his grasp. "Sorry, your highness."

"Stop it," he hissed. "If you think this was easy for me you're sadly mistaken. Now one of us needs to make sure she keeps her end of the bargain."

It was at least two hours before we were summoned into the throne room, Helig bowing low before leaving us. The queen looked down, her gaze trained on Harold. "I trust you had breakfast?" she asked him.

"I did, and it was very good."

She smiled. "I am glad. Now as to Maeve's magic, it will take some time before it is fully returned. I cannot work a miracle so quickly."

"Thank you, Aine," Harold said, bowing.

"You are most welcome, Harold. Now if you will excuse me I have matters to attend to." And without another word she rose, walked gracefully down from the dais, and exited the room.

I turned to Harold. "That was short and sweet."

He stared at me without expression and turned toward the door. I hurried after him.

We were halfway down the hill before Harold spoke again. "What you did is nearly unforgiveable," he began, his eyes forward. "You put me in an untenable position and now there will be a baby." His eyes met mine, the bleakness in his giving me a shiver. "I can't let that child walk though this life without a father."

"Are you sure she's pregnant?"

He stared at me his lips narrowing into a thin line. "We made sure of it, Maeve. The queen is quite aware of such things."

This meant they had not only done it once, but perhaps several times. I felt sick to my stomach. "I'm so sorry, Harold. I don't know what I was thinking. Yes, I do. I was thinking only of myself. The consequences of this never occurred to me, other than worrying that you'd fall in love with her or she'd bewitch you."

He shook his head. "She isn't like that, Maeve. She is the last of the royal line of elves and hasn't had any affection in decades. I felt so sorry for her that I was in tears at one point."

I wanted to make a snarky remark but his expression told me not to. Excusing my shallow behavior was impossible since there was something in me that wanted to continue; I was jealous and hurt that he'd had such deep feelings for her so quickly. "At least now she'll have an heir," I finally mumbled. "What happened to her people?"

"Long ago, and I mean nearly a century, there was a battle between her people, the Tel-quessir, and the Sluagh. The Tel-quessir won, but in the process there was a disease that wiped most of them out. The one you called Spriggan is part of the Gwyllion, another race that was on the brink of extinction. They were happy to allow Aine to rule them since she is kind and generous and has an open heart. At the time she built this castle there were nearly a hundred of her kind, but over the years they have sickened and died. There are barely twenty here now. The Tel-quessir are elven in nature and tend to have frail constitutions."

"I don't know what to say other than I wish I'd never offered the idea as a solution. It was thoughtless and stupid. Can you love me again?"

Harold turned, his eyes glistening. "I never stopped loving you, Maeve."

Despite his words I had the sense that something had changed between us—something essential. It was an hour before I ventured into another conversation with him, his stern expression and focus in the distance putting me off. "Did the queen mention why the Sluagh were running around killing people, or why we were attacked?"

"I didn't ask her, but she did say there's a war brewing and that humans should stay out of it. The Sluagh have only recently returned and they want Otherworld all to themselves. I guess their numbers have grown and where they were living can no longer sustain them."

"Does that mean the Tel-quessir and the Gwyllion are out-numbered?"

Harold nodded without looking at me. "I fear that if humans do not get involved they will be wiped out."

"Why did she say not to?"

He finally turned, his eyes dark and remote. "It is a faery fight and she's worried that humans will lose their lives over it."

I looked down, not wanting to see the hostile expression on his face. "And yet if we don't get involved we could have the Sluagh running things here. That doesn't seem good to me."

"I agree. I plan to speak with MacCuill about it. Kenneth may come in handy very soon."

"Harold, you can't be serious."

"Why not? I have a warrior part. I've been bored ever since the conflict here ended. Kenneth can call an army together."

"But—the house, our baby."

"This won't happen in the next few days, Maeve. Your house will be completed by the time it begins."

I noticed his use of 'your' house, a deep chill running through me. I didn't say anything else as I followed him into the snow-covered forests of the lower elevations. I shivered and pulled my cloak back on, worried about what the future held. If I did get my powers back I could be instrumental in the conflict, but did I want to get involved in the Fae war? But my worst worry was about Harold and the baby who would soon be born.

By the time we reached the castle I was worn to a frazzle. It had been three days with no hint of my powers coming back, the baby had been fussy the entire trip because of my lack of milk, and Harold's attitude toward me had not lifted. We'd barely spoken since our conversation about the Fae war.

MacCuill took one look at me and grabbed hold of my arm. "What has happened, Maeve? You look worse than when you left."

I glanced at Harold, who stood with his back to me, staring out a window toward the sea. "It was a long trip. The faery queen promised that I will get my magic back, but she said it will take some time."

"What did you have to do for that?" he asked.

I shook my head. "It's a long story. Can I go lie down? I feel too tired to think."

"Of course." The druid led me to our room and opened the door. "I'll speak with Harold while you rest. When you wake come to the dining hall. You look as though you could use a good meal."

Once I was alone I was finally able to let down my guard. I pulled my sleeping baby from the pack and laid her gently on the quilt before allowing the pent-up tears to flow.

CHAPTER
TWENTY-FOUR

Harold felt a coldness toward Maeve he'd never had before. When he looked at her he was astounded by his lack of affection and his anger. He knew he was not under a spell—the queen didn't need to bewitch him to get what she wanted. He wasn't in love with Aine, but he did feel a deep affection for her and everything she'd been through. She had lived more than a hundred years without a partner. He was glad he'd been with her and hoped that everything would go well with the pregnancy. But underneath all that he felt responsible. For him it wasn't possible to conceive a child and walk away. It pulled at him and took him away from everything he knew and thought he loved. Yes, he had Airy, and she was a delight. He loved her with all his heart. But what did he feel for Maeve? What had changed so drastically that he had turned away from her? And more importantly, would his feelings return.

"Harold, what has happened to exhaust Maeve?"

He turned from the window to face the druid. "She made a bargain with the Tel-quessir queen. In exchange for the queen restoring her powers she gave me to Aine for one night. I was supposed to give her a child."

The druid's eyes narrowed. "And did you?"

"Yes, I believe I did."

"And this is the reason Maeve looks as though she's been through a war?"

Harold let out a long sigh. "Something happened between us, MacCuill. I can't explain it, but I'm having a hard time connecting with her right now."

"So, she is worried you don't love her. Did you fall in love with the queen? If memory serves, Aine is very beautiful."

Harold shook his head. "It isn't that. Maeve didn't consult me before offering me up. I felt used and disrespected. And her attitude about other things has been unfeeling as well. I don't know what's gotten into her."

"Could it be jealousy?"

"Possibly, but it wasn't jealousy that caused her to give me to the queen as though I was nothing more than her plaything."

MacCuill stared into the distance. "I'm not trying to excuse her, but this could be a residual effect of the spell being removed and the loss of her magic. It has placed her in a very vulnerable position. She's also given birth recently. She might need to speak with someone."

"Like a therapist?"

MacCuill smiled. "We don't have those here. No. I meant more like an understanding woman, or man, who could listen and offer advice."

"That's the definition of a therapist," Harold muttered. "Who comes to mind?"

"The moon goddess would be a good one—or Airmid."

"Not Rea?"

"Rea is too closely involved with the two of you. I'm afraid she couldn't be objective."

Harold nodded.

"Now, Harold, I can tell there is more on your mind than Maeve. What do you need to talk about?"

Once they were seated in the dining hall with food in front of them Harold proceeded to tell the druid about the war brewing between the Fae. "I want to help. I can gather an army together and fight for the Tel-quessir and the Gwyllion. Even though the queen told me to stay out of it, they need us. They are but one hundred strong, and from what I heard the Sluagh have at least a thousand."

MacCuill steepled his fingers, lost in thought. He finally nodded and looked up. "As you know the conclave here is in process of reorganizing. I am in charge until such time as we pick another ruler. I would like to offer my help, but if this happens before we've settled our business it could cause problems. I am sure the Wildmen would stand with you, especially if Maeve's powers were reinstated and she led them. The villagers will listen to you if you want to recruit their help. I think you have many at your disposal."

"I was hoping for your help, MacCuill. You were instrumental in the last war."

MacCuill grimaced. "I am getting too old for this, Harold. I'll support you as much as I can, but as I said, it depends on when."

"The queen thinks it's imminent, but that could mean months. The Sluagh are already disrupting life in the villages. They've attacked several. That has to stop."

"Get your army together. Once you've established a force come and talk to me again. Maybe by then we'll be in a better place to discuss it." MacCuill turned as Maeve walked toward them, the baby in her arms. "Did you get some rest?"

Maeve glanced at Harold. "A little. I think Airy has colic—she's been fussy for a week now."

"Sit by me," MacCuill said, patting the bench next to him. "Have some food, Maeve." He pointed to the array of meats and cheeses, pickles and apples laid out on the table.

Harold watched her sit down, noticing the wary look in her eyes. He had a moment of guilt at his behavior toward her. When she held the baby out he took her, settling Airy on his lap.

"Did you make a plan?" Maeve asked him, before putting a piece of cheese in her mouth.

"We did. I've decided to take you back to Tiadan. I'll get the men to continue work on the house while I scout Otherworld for recruits."

"It might have been nice if you'd run this by me, Harold. If my powers come back I might be some use, you know."

"That's rich after what you—"

MacCuill held up his hand. "Children, children—quit squabbling. What I suggested to Harold, Maeve, is for you to have a talk with someone you trust. You've gone through a lot these past weeks, and I'm sure you're—"

"What did Harold tell you?" she interrupted. "That I've turned into a thoughtless bitch?" She got to her feet and grabbed Airy out of Harold's arms. "I would appreciate it if you didn't discuss me behind my back." She stalked to the front door and opened it, slamming it closed behind her.

"She's touchy," MacCuill said, turning to Harold. "I've never seen her like this."

"That's what I was trying to tell you."

"Maybe a visit to Finna and Alex might be in order. Maeve's mother is a wise woman and understands the hormonal changes that come with childbirth; perhaps that's all it is."

"If I suggest it I doubt she'll go for it. Maybe you could mention it?"

MacCuill nodded. "I'll give her some time alone and then go talk to her."

"While you're doing that I'm going to go search out Duncan. He's still in touch with a lot of the men who followed Maeve in the last war."

When Harold left a short time later he could see Maeve in the distance walking slowly along the shore. Her head was bent, the dark hood of her cloak covering her bright hair. Sadness moved through him when he tried to recollect his feelings for her.

The sky had darkened again, a storm approaching. He was getting sick of winter, especially after the time spent up in the temperate mountains. He pulled his coat closed, turning inland to find Argyll and make the trek to Duncan's house. He hoped the rain or snow would hold off until he returned.

When Harold returned to the castle several hours later the wind was blowing directly off the water, stinging his face with tiny ice pellets. He pulled up his collar and bent forward, riding as quickly as he dared. Duncan had assured him that he had friends in high places and that raising an army would be child's play. Harold wasn't so sure. There were many in Otherworld who did not trust the Fae and would have nothing to do with them. Fighting in what basically was a Fae civil war did not appeal to them. It would take a lot of education before they could be brought on board. He let out a sigh, his thoughts going to Aine and the tears they'd both shed during their one night together. He had to do this for her. If he didn't she and the mountain Fae she ruled over would not survive.

When he reached the Druid castle he was stiff with cold, glad to see a fire burning in the dining hall. He went to sit in front of the warm flames, his thoughts scattering from one topic to another. When he heard footsteps he turned to see MacCuill approaching with an unfamiliar druid. "Have you talked with Maeve?" he asked.

MacCuill shook his head. "I couldn't find her. Is she sleeping?"

"I just got back--haven't been to our room."

A look of worry appeared on the druid's face. "I think you should check on her, Harold."

"Why? What's happened?"

"Just check. I followed her footprints for a mile and a half before I turned back."

Harold left his spot by the fire and hurried deeper into the castle. When he reached the room the door was open. "Maeve?" he called, pushing it wide. There was no one there, and when he searched further he saw that Maeve's and the baby's things had been taken. He tore back to the hall, bursting into the conversation between the two men. "She's gone."

CHAPTER TWENTY-FIVE

The shoreline curved, a forested hill on my left obscuring the view in that direction. From a distance this bay resembled a shell, the pale sand in steep contrast to the deep jewel tone of the sea. I turned to gaze on Arianrhod's castle of ice glinting in the dusky light. Caer Sidi was a magical place and yet I couldn't feel it. I had no idea what I was doing or where I was going, only that I couldn't stand being around Harold. He hadn't said two words to me in three days. And as far as touching me he hadn't gotten near enough to do so even when we were sleeping side by side. I had cried every tear I had and tried to come up with some idea of how to reach him. But in the end I knew I simply had to leave.

His plan to take me back to Tiadan did not sit well, especially with him going off in warrior mode to save Aine and her people. I felt crushed by his dedication to her. I only hoped that eventually my powers would begin to creep back and give me the strength I needed; right now I felt more alone than any time in my life.

As I walked further and further from the druid castle I lost track of time, and when I finally registered how long I'd been gone a shroud of dark had closed in around me. The moon appeared, the lack of cloud bringing with it an arctic blast that set my teeth on edge. I was glad I had thought to dress Airy in the warm wool Rea had given her. Since it was too far back to the castle I headed away from the sea, hoping to find an abandoned shack or barn where Airy and I could shelter for the night.

I had not gone far when I realized I'd entered the enchanted forest—not the best place to be. Airy woke suddenly and let out a piercing scream, startling me into a crouching position as though her shriek heralded some deadly beast. But all was quiet. Too quiet, I thought to myself, peering into the shadows. "Do you need to eat, sweet one?" I whispered, trying to slow my wildly beating heart. Of course she didn't answer.

I moved on carefully, only too aware of what could happen. I'd become lost here in the past and voices had led me up one trail and down another—paths that led nowhere. The trees were gnarled, with tangled branches that twined above my head, blocking the sky and distant light of the moon. Roots loomed up out of the earth like fat serpents ready to strike. My exhaustion was making me imagine things. I was hopelessly lost, and if I didn't find a place to spend the night soon we would end up out in the open in a forest that came alive at night with unseen and dangerous creatures. I had to get a grip, I told myself sternly.

But when I heard a sudden raucous caw and then another and another, followed by the whoosh of wings, I completely freaked out. I pulled off the pack and held the baby beneath me, sure that any second those horrible flying creatures would attack. It was quiet for a moment and I dared open my eyes, peering over my shoulder to see where they'd gone. They hadn't gone anywhere, many dark eyes peering at me from tree branches, an enormous bird on the ground right next to me. But when I looked into his beady eye, I did not see the malevolence I'd expected. Instead he seemed to be trying to communicate something—trouble was I couldn't receive his message. Airy began to chortle and coo, her hands going out toward the bird who sat still, watching her. My baby was not afraid of him. "What do you want?" I whispered.

The bird moved his wings out and rose into the air as though pulled by some unseen force. He clacked his beak noisily and flew to a tree branch some distance away. The other birds were silent now, waiting. I rose and moved toward my guide, following as he led us through the forest. When we arrived at a broken-down shack I breathed a sigh of relief. The door hung by one hinge and I pushed it wide, finding a warm and relatively clean space. "Thank you," I called out. I heard their answering raspy calls and then the beat and whir of many wings as they lifted and disappeared.

Once I pulled the door closed and settled against a wall with the baby on my lap it was so dark I couldn't see my hand in front of my face. Nothing to do but sleep, I thought to myself, hoping I would be safe. But the ravens had led me here and I had the good sense to know they were on my side. I closed my eyes and let sleep take me.

In the morning my neck was stiff, but other than that we'd both survived. When I looked down at Airy she had a finger in her mouth sucking while she slept. I placed her on my cloak and stood to stretch. What was I thinking coming this far? Harold must be worried sick. But then I remembered. Harold was more than likely on his way to gather his army together for the queen, his thoughts as far from me as they could get.

I was attempting to retrace my steps when I heard Harold calling my name. "I'm here!" I shouted, trying to move in the direction of his voice.

When he burst from under the trees I stumbled backward and would have fallen had he not grabbed my arm. But when my gaze met his it was not happiness I saw on his face.

"What in hell do you think you're doing, Maeve? MacCuill and I have been searching all bloody night! If you want to kill yourself, fine, but don't take Airy along."

"Oh, thanks very much for that," I said, brushing off my clothes and trying to seem dignified and together. "I was merely taking a walk and lost track of time."

His eyes narrowed. "And ended up in the enchanted forest in the middle of the night? How stupid is that?"

"About as stupid as you..." I stopped when tears welled. I had promised myself I would not cry again.

He peered at me through the gloom of early morning. "Me what?"

I glared at him. "You don't love me anymore, Harold. Admit it and move on. Airy and I will survive."

Harold stared at me without speaking. "Maeve, I—"

"Don't try and make me feel better. Let's just make a clean break now, before we hurt each other any more."

"Maeve, I don't want to break up." He laughed wryly. "Breaking up is a strange term to be using in Otherworld with a woman who's holding my baby in her arms."

"Something happened between you and Aine that seems deeper than one night of sex." When he began to protest I held up my hand. "I don't know what it was, and maybe you don't either, but it's affected us, and until we get it sorted out we can't move forward—at least not together. I'm willing to take some time apart, but I don't know where to go." Damn it I was crying again and this time it didn't show any signs of slowing down. When Harold pulled me into his arms I sobbed against him.

"It'll be all right," he said, stroking my tangled hair. "We'll figure it out."

When the baby let out a wail of complaint from where she rested against my back the moment came to an end. I pulled away and removed the pack to feed her.

Harold knelt next to me. "That is a beautiful sight," he whispered, his fingers running across her red curls.

"It would be if I had enough to satisfy her," I muttered, moving her to the other side.

He looked up, his gaze meeting mine. "I did a lot of thinking last night while I was searching for you. You're right about Aine, but it isn't what you think. I'm not in love with her. You hurt me, Maeve, and made me feel small—as though I was an underling you could manipulate. I went along because I was forced to. But Aine is real—we talked a lot and I got to know her. You can't expect me to have sex with a woman and not connect with her," he said gently. "Is that what you imagined would happen?"

I let out a deep sigh. "I don't know what I was thinking, Harold. The idea came to me and I ran with it. All I could focus on was getting my powers back."

"And the child—did you give any thought to the baby Aine and I conceived?"

I shook my head, fighting tears. "Definitely not."

"And yet you knew that's what she wanted." Harold's eyes welled. "You acted like a spoiled child. What you forced me to do has consequences. You do realize that I will always be connected with her now? You and I will never be able to go back to the way it once was between us."

I was sobbing again and this time it felt like my heart would break. I wished with all my being that we could go back in time and change that one instant when I offered him to the faery queen. "I'm so sorry," I blubbered, my head in my hands. "I wish it could be undone. Can we at least try now, or do you want to go our separate ways?"

Harold's glittering eyes met mine. "Deep down I still love you, but it will take some time to get over this. You'll have to be patient. Now please, don't take off like this again."

Once the baby had taken all I had to give Harold helped me to my feet, holding her while I retrieved the pack from the ground. I followed him through the shadowy forest, wondering how long before we were back to normal, or if we'd ever be. I felt heavy with sadness and furious with myself for what I'd done.

Once we reached the castle Harold left me at the front door and hurried off to find MacCuill. It wasn't locked and I made my way to our room and sank down on the bed. My hands were tingling and I wondered if I'd strained a muscle in my neck. Before I could stop myself I was face down, crying my eyes out. A voice in my head screamed, *why are you so stupid? What were you thinking? How will you ever get him back?* And then Aine loomed up in my mind, her belly straining against the silky fabric of the gorgeous gown she wore. *What had I done?* She would always be in Harold's heart, and when she gave birth he would go to her. Nothing would ever be the same. "At least I have you," I whispered, giving Airy a kiss on the top of her head. She gurgled and held out one fat baby hand. But Airy was another issue I didn't want to face. I was too thin to make milk, and it was only a matter of time before I would have to find a wet nurse.

When Harold returned an hour later he announced that we would leave for Tiadan the next morning. I didn't argue.

CHAPTER TWENTY-SIX

In Tiadan Harold made arrangements with his workers before saying a cursory farewell. He didn't look back as he rode away on Argyll, his sword hanging by his side. I'd never had a chance to tell him about my experience with the ravens; I was sure that whatever had attacked him in the barn in Tiadan had not been the dark birds. From what I knew now, I was sure it had been the flying creatures, the Sluagh.

Our trip from Caer Sidi had been made in virtual silence, and when I attempted to snuggle at night he turned his back. So much for loving me, I thought. How long would he punish me for one moment of foolishness? Unfortunately that one moment would now stretch into a lifetime that excluded me.

It was three weeks of me moping around, barely eating and sitting for hours staring at the sea before Tannith forced it out of me. "I can see by yer face and Harold's actions that somethin' is not right between ye," she began. "It seems to me that whatever is goin' on now is beyond what happened with Gan Ceanach. If ye want to talk I'm here, Maeve, and a good listener. I've had my share of love troubles and I know a thing or two."

I hesitated, not wanting to revisit the painful subject, but even if I didn't talk about it, it was always on my mind. And with Harold gone off to make arrangements to fight for the Tel-quessir I had a very bad feeling about what he might be up to. Visions of the two of them together loomed in my mind, making me heartsick.

"Is it about the war or your powers? I thought you said you'd been havin' some twinges of magic again."

I met her worried gaze. "I've been having a few visions, but I don't know if they're real or my overactive imagination."

"What are they? Maybe I can help."

I shook my head and removed the crying baby from my empty breast. "If I tell you the story I'll be a mess, Tannith. I did something very stupid and it's come back to haunt me."

"'Tis nae good to hold pain in, Maeve. Sharing with a friend can relieve it—believe me, I've been there."

I jiggled the baby on my knee trying to settle her, but the cries only grew louder.

Tannith took her from me. "The wee one is hungry. You are not eating properly and your milk is dryin' up. We can supplement with goat's milk, but if you wish to continue ye must put on some weight." She put her finger in the baby's mouth to soothe her as she bustled around the kitchen to finagle a way to give her the goat's milk. She rigged up loose muslin and turned it into a little funnel that she poured a small amount of milk into. When she pressed the pointed end into the baby's mouth Airy drank greedily. "This will work,"

188

Tannith said, handing her to me. "Maybe some porridge is in order as well."

Yule, as Harold had called it, had come and gone. Airy was nearly four months old. And the house he'd promised was yet to be finished enough to move into. The weather had been miserable of late, and the men were unable to work on it, instead huddling in their houses by the fire to escape the cold winter blast that had descended on Tiadan. I imagined Harold in the temperate climate with the Fae, a sick jealousy winding its way through my belly. He hadn't touched me in over a month. Was he lying with Aine right now? I shook my head, trying to get rid of the upsetting thoughts.

"Maeve, please tell me what's wrong."

I looked up from the baby in my lap. "Harold—" As soon as his name was out of my mouth I was crying.

Tannith came close, placing her arm around my shoulder. "Unburden yourself, child."

"I forced him to—I made a bargain with the faery queen. In exchange for spending one night with Harold she would give me back my powers."

"And she can do this?"

I shrugged. "She said she could. But the point is I didn't ask Harold before I offered him to her. And now—" I looked up again and wiped my eyes. "And now she's pregnant, or at least I think she is; it was part of the bargain."

Tannith frowned, staring into the distance. "The bargain was that Harold would give her a child, is that it?"

I nodded. "She's nearly the last of her race, and certainly the last of the elven royal line. She wants an heir."

"And what did Harold say about it?"

"He didn't say anything. He went with her and I didn't see him again until the following day."

Tannith's gaze met mine. "Why didn't he say no?"

I opened my mouth and closed it, pondering her question. "I guess he knew how much I wanted my powers back."

Tannith stood and began to pace. "You feel a terrible guilt for what you foisted on him, and yet he is a grown man and could have refused. And if he had, some other agreement might have been arranged."

"I hadn't thought of that. But now he and Aine are forever connected. And I know for a fact that when that baby is born he'll be by her side."

"You feel you've lost him and you blame it all on yourself."

"It's all my fault. If I hadn't—"

"Consider this, Maeve. Harold made his own decision to lie with the queen. As to bein' around for the baby, that is not his responsibility. If he chooses to take it on then that is his prerogative, but it doesn't have anything to do with you."

"It does because he doesn't feel the same way about me anymore!" I cried out.

"First of all you must let go of the guilt you've placed on yourself. It is causing you to lose weight, and if you aren't careful you will become ill. Once Harold gets back you need to have a long talk with him. He's hurt you terribly with his blame and self-righteous attitude. He needs to be honest with himself."

I had a momentary lifting of the heaviness I'd been carrying. "So even though I offered him to the queen, you think I don't bear all the guilt for what happened?"

Tannith shook her head. "No, I don't Maeve. And if he continues to browbeat you over it I'd give him hell."

I wiped the last tears from my cheeks. "He doesn't browbeat, he just doesn't touch me or show any affection. And now with this war I fear what may be happening between them."

"Whatever happens it isn't your fault. He is making his own decisions about his actions. You and Harold have a baby together and I know he loves ye—I've seen it shining from his eyes. Try and take care of yourself so that when he comes back you are strong and look the best ye possibly can. When your powers return you'll feel yourself again, I'm sure of it. Dinna let him strip you of your self-esteem."

I smiled. "Sounds like you've had your share of jerk men," I said.

Tannith laughed. "That I have. It is good to be too old now to worry about it."

I really looked at her for the first time, noticing her flushed cheeks, the light in her eyes. She was in her fifties and full of life, hardly too old to be in a relationship. "You aren't too old for love."

"You are sweet, but who would have me?"

I smiled. "I'm sure there are many men who would be happy to share your bed."

She blushed bright red. "Go on with ye, then," she said, flustered, turning to her cheeses.

I bundled Airy into her wool and pulled on my cloak. "I'm going for a walk."

"Don't tarry, lass. There is a storm comin' in, mark my words."

I was on the cliff edge when the wind came up, blowing back the hood of my cloak and taking my breath away. I loved storms like this, the energy they produced, and the electricity that seemed to sizzle though my veins when I was out in it. A vision presented itself to me as clear as day. Harold was in the presence of the queen, bowed down on my knee. They were in conference about the army he was raising. I clearly heard her say, *"I will accept your help, but you must bow to my command. There is too much at stake here to have a human in charge."*

"I will, my queen," Harold replied. And then the vision was gone. This was definitely my clairvoyance returning. And from what I saw the relationship was purely a formal one. Could I trust that this was the truth?

The night before we left the druid castle he'd slept in another room and he'd made no move since then to show he cared. The day he left Tiadan he hadn't bothered to kiss me, or even smile, barely saying goodbye before turning his back to ride away. Since my conversation with Tannith I no longer felt the guilt I'd taken on, the sense that I'd wronged him. What I'd done was inexcusable, but his going along with it was nearly as bad. The wind whistled by, giving me an instant earache. I pulled the baby close and struggled against the gale back to the house.

"Your powers are returnin'," Tannith said when I relayed what I'd seen.

I stuffed a piece of bread and cheese in my mouth, nodding my agreement.

She laughed, watching me. "And your appetite too! Soon you can curtail the goat's milk and feed wee Airy yourself."

"I hope so. I've missed it."

"Did ye know that the men have gone off to fight with Harold? 'Tis why your house is unfinished."

"No, I didn't. When did they leave?"

"A week ago, from what I hear. The war will keep them away from their new bairns and wives for a long while, I suspect."

"I hope I see Harold soon. I'm missing him now."

"He'll be back when he can, but in the meantime ye have some more weight to gain and a baby to raise. Let's hope the war doesn't come anywhere around here."

I thought about that. I'd been instrumental in the last war, my healing abilities and clairvoyance allowing me to help in ways I was unable to do now. Unless—unless the magic returned. And if it did would I leave my baby with Tannith and go fight by Harold's side? I saw us as we'd been in the last war, riding side by side and discussing our plans. It was hard to imagine it now, as though our estranged relationship wouldn't allow it. We were no longer a team.

CHAPTER
TWENTY-SEVEN

Harold led the group he'd recruited up the mountain path, leaving them in a large clearing before heading on foot to speak with the queen. So far he'd raised nearly one hundred able-bodied men, somehow convincing them that it was in their best interest to fight for her cause. Many of them had not made the trip up here, instead heading off to find others to march with them. They would need hundreds more if they were to defeat the Sluagh.

When he was ushered into the castle he had a moment of deja vu, remembering his last time here, the night spent with Aine. Had his seed found purchase? And then he laughed to himself at the archaic phrase that had appeared in his mind. Kenneth was at the fore. The door was opened by a tall graceful faery who had to be Tel-quessir. "The queen is expecting you," she said, leading him through the dining hall.

"Harold, it is good to see you again," the queen said when he entered the throne room. She turned to the faery standing behind him. "And thank you, Elora. Will you alert the kitchen that we have an additional guest?" Elora nodded and bowed before backing out the door. The queen turned to Harold, a smile on her lovely features. "As you can see I am in a delicate condition at the moment." She stood to show off her protruding belly.

Harold's jaw dropped. "It seems too big for how recently I—we—"

"Faery's have a shorter gestation period. I will give birth in the spring, if I'm not mistaken."

Harold counted up the time since he'd been here. It had been three months. "How many moons?"

"It takes six moons for a faery to gestate. Now stop staring at my less than attractive figure and let us get down to business."

Harold did not think her figure was unattractive, in fact quite the opposite. Her cheeks were rosy, her eyes shining, and she looked in the peak of health. "I think you look more lovely than ever," he said, lowering his head in a respectful bow.

Ignoring his comment she carefully descended from the dais and walked toward him. She looped her arm through his. "We will meet with my advisors. They wait for us beneath the castle."

The door they entered was one Harold hadn't noticed, set into a deep recess. When they entered the dark stairwell Aine waved her hand, producing many twinkling lights that moved with them as they descended. The air grew more humid the further they went, the spiraling stairs leading them deeper into the mountain.

"It is not often I walk these steps," she said. "I am glad to have your arm for support."

"Glad to be of service."

"Your service is appreciated," she teased, one hand resting on her belly. "How is your mate--your baby?"

"They're both fine. I left them in Tiadan—do you know it?"

"Tiadan. It lies on the edge of the Yew forest?"

Harold nodded, catching her under the elbow when she stumbled. "I'm building a house for us, but—"

"But, what? It is a lovely place with a wonderful view."

"Maeve and I—we—"

The queen paused to turn to him. "I hope I am not the cause of a rift between you. What happened between us was merely a means to an end."

"I feel a connection with you now that you carry my child. This is not something I take lightly."

"And yet you have a wife and a child of your own. I am capable of taking care of myself, Harold. I would never have lain with you if I thought it would cause you to abandon your own life."

"I'm not talking of abandoning Maeve, I am only suggesting that when the time comes I will be here for you— that is, barring the war and what might be going on."

"Harold, I would never ask that of you. I have people who look after me. I am queen."

"You don't have to ask. I want to be here."

"And how does Maeve feel about this?"

Harold turned away as Maeve's distraught face appeared in his mind. "I haven't told her but I'm sure she'll be jealous."

"Of course she would be. I beg you to consider your decisions regarding this baby very carefully. I did not do this to keep you by my side—quite the contrary. I am fond of you, but you do not have to be present in my child's life, nor do you bear any responsibility for him or her."

Harold met her clear gaze. "What if I want to be involved?"

The queen turned back to the stairs, lifting her long skirt with one hand, her other hand holding tightly to his arm. "That is of course, your choice, but if it is disturbing to Maeve, I would show caution."

The room they reached at the bottom was without windows, lit torches set into sconces lighting up the yellowish stone and casting flickering shadows across the many faces of the men and women seated around the table. They ranged from small and gnome-like to tall with pointed ears, and three who were blonde and built like Aine.

"This is Harold, the man I spoke to you about. He has offered his services as a warrior and recruiter of men to fight for our cause. We owe him a debt for the army he has already raised. Now we will fill him in on our own strategy and put our heads together."

By the time the meeting was over Harold's head was swimming—so many differing ideas, so much arguing and shouting. He had kept silent, listening instead of trying to put forth his ideas. He had to get the lay of the land first.

After a shared meal in the dining hall, catered by the queen's attentive wait staff, he and Aine returned to the throne room. The panes of glass reflected the darkness that had fallen and he realized that he would have to spend the night. He was about to mention this when the queen took him by the hand and led him through the door and up the stairs to her bedchamber.

"You may make love to me without fear," she told him as she removed her long silky dress. He stared at her new curves, her full and rounded breasts, the belly that held his baby. He was immediately aroused.

In the bed he pulled her hair back from her neck to kiss her pale skin. "Am I your only lover?" he murmured.

"Yes, Harold. I find that I am increasingly in need of a man these days, as though the pregnancy has brought my long repressed desire to the surface. I had planned to keep you at arm's length, but I find that I am unable to deny myself. I only hope that what we do together will not affect your relationship with Maeve. Are you capable of a purely physical liaison?"

"I don't view my time with you as purely physical, Aine. I am deeply fond of you and enjoy all our interactions."

"So diplomatic!" she laughed. She turned to him, her lips parting as she pressed her mouth to his.

Harold pulled her close, feeling her fragility and the press of her belly as they coupled.

It was late morning before he left her bed. A sweet tenderness moved through him as paused to look down on her. Her golden hair fanned out on the pillow, one arm flung behind her head. When he brushed his lips against hers, her eyelids fluttered, but she didn't wake. They hadn't had much sleep.

In between the lovemaking they'd talked, and his admiration for her had grown. She was a benevolent and caring leader, a strong woman who could lead an army as well as delegate. He hoped he had convinced her to steer clear of it all, at least until the baby came. Sometime during the long night he'd recognized that it was Kenneth who was making love to her and Kenneth who was planning to lead her army. And this realization made him feel better about what he was doing. But still he felt that he'd betrayed Maeve and wondered how he could justify this. Was he falling in love with Aine?

He dressed and strapped on his sword before heading from her bedchamber. There was no one about when he went by the dining hall. He left the castle and strode down the hill to where he'd left his men. But when he got to the meadow he was met with a bloody and grizzly scene. At least forty of his men lay dead, the rest gone. He searched through the contorted and hacked up bodies, trying hard not to retch. There was no one left alive. He recognized many of the dead as friends, villagers he'd coaxed to come here. The Sluagh had come while he was happily ensconced in the queen's bed, slaughtering as many as they could. He let out a hollow scream that reverberated against the craggy cliffs before retching into the dirt. "What have I done?" he shouted, holding his head in his hands. And then he turned away, sprinting back to the castle to rouse the queen.

By the time the queen was dressed Harold had contacted her advisors and a crowd had gathered in the front hall. "I say we go find the plundering bastards," Harold growled in his Kenneth voice, "and kill every last one of them."

"Let us not be hasty," Aine said. "If they are close we will be safer to stay in the castle. Outside we'll be easy prey to the ones who fly."

Harold frowned, staring at her. "I can't sit here and do nothing."

"Find your horse and track them, but be careful. They are vicious as evidenced by what you described."

"We need to bury what's left of them," Harold muttered.

Aine shook her head. "Let the ravens and crows pick their bones. The dead won't mind."

Harold was about to protest when she began to speak to the assembled crowd. "We will use the tunnels beneath the mountain to scout. No one is to leave the safety of the mountains until I say so. They far outman us at this point, and until we have a large enough army we will have to use stealth as our weapon. Now go and bring back news of whatever you find."

She turned to Harold. "Why are you still here? I ordered you to take your horse and track them."

Harold opened his mouth and closed it. Gone was the sensuous woman who had lain beneath him during the night, replaced with an implacable goddess warrior. "Yes, my queen," he said, bowing. He turned and left the castle, his hand on his sword. Hopefully Argyll had not been hurt during the attack.

CHAPTER
TWENTY-EIGHT

"**H**e had sex with her."

Tannith turned from the bread bowl. "What did ye say?"

I placed my hand on my fast beating heart. "I had a vision of Harold and Aine together in a four-poster bed."

"Are ye quite sure it was real? It could have been your worry causin' it."

"It was real, Tannith. He made love to her again." I turned away to hide my tears.

"Tis difficult to see Harold in this role, Maeve. Could he be possessed or under a spell?"

I shook my head. "The other part is even worse. The men who were with him—his recruits? Most of them are dead. The creatures with the wings killed them."

Tannith put a hand on her heart, bending over as if she'd run a mile. "Many are villagers from here—my friends. Are ye quite sure?"

"I saw the scene of death in my mind as though it was right in front of my eyes." I paced the room keeping an ear out for the baby who slept on the bed upstairs. Both of us had had a restless night. "I don't know what to do."

"What *can* ye do? There is nothing for it but to wait. I am sick inside at the idea of it. They are not our kind—why do human lives have to be wasted for the Fae?"

I wanted to say, because they are living beings, but I couldn't because I was wondering the same thing. I was no longer the person I'd been a year ago when I fought side by side with the Oillteil and the Wildmen, healing them when they were hurt. Something fundamental had changed since Gan Ceanach had taken my powers, and what was happening with the queen and Harold was only a part of it. For the first time since I'd been in Otherworld I wondered if I should go back to the States.

"What are ye thinkin', lass?" Tannith asked, gazing at me.

"Why do you ask?"

"Because I have never seen that particular look on yer face before, and it is frightenin' to behold."

I laughed, trying to hide what was going through my mind. "I have clairvoyance now, and telepathy, although I haven't truly tested it. Do you think I'll be able to move from one place to another again—through the ether? And if I get all my magic back does that mean the Fae won't have it?"

"I canna answer that, but I figure they will have it as well. But since you are the Willow, yours will be stronger." She smiled.

"I can help Harold if I choose to, but I wonder if it wouldn't be better for us to stay out of this Fae war."

"My sentiments exactly," Tannith said, plunging her hands into the bowl of rough ground flour, butter and goat's milk.

"And yet there's danger to all the inhabitants of Otherworld if the Sluagh take over."

"We will fight them if they attack us, Maeve. That isn't the same as fightin' for the Fae."

I thought about that for a moment. "But what if the Sluagh wipe them all out? The Tel-quessir and the Gwyllion are the good ones, and can't defend themselves."

Tannith threw up her dough-covered hands, sending bits of flour flying. "I canna think about it all; it makes my head hurt. But I do have a suggestion on another topic. Since Harold is gone and we don't know where Dougal and Iain have gone off to, why don't we hire a few women from town and between us we can finish buildin' your house?"

I gazed at her in surprise. "That's a great idea!" A second later I heard the unmistakable wail of my baby and hurried upstairs.

It was many weeks before I had another vision, and this was one I couldn't turn away from. I had no more tears as I replayed it in my mind.

CHAPTER
TWENTY-NINE

"Yes, of course I like having you here, Harold. And as far as our nights, they give me much pleasure. But I worry about our plans to fight the Sluagh. Spending time in my bedchamber is not bringing us any closer to solving the problems."

Harold stared into her emerald eyes, feeling mesmerized as always. "I may be falling in love with you," he murmured, moving to kiss her perfect earlobe.

The queen pulled away and rose from the bed to retrieve her silk robe. Harold watched her pull it closed and tie it above where her belly bulged. She was close to the time of delivery and he planned to be here for the birth.

"I feel the same," she said. "But I would not call it love. We are two people working toward a common goal and we happen to have a certain chemistry between us. Have you given any thought to Maeve or your baby? They must be missing you."

Harold frowned, not wanting to think about them or the guilt that rose up when he did. "What I feel for them doesn't change anything, Aine. As I've told you, I have a sort of split personality, and Kenneth seems to want to remain here with you."

"And what about Harold?"

He stared at the mullioned window where dusky dawn light filtered through the wavy glass. "Harold be damned until we've beaten back the Sluagh."

Aine laughed. "Shall I call you Kenneth, then?"

"If you wish, my queen," he said, rolling out of bed.

When he moved toward her she backed away. "I know that look and now is not the time. It is morning and we both have our duties to perform."

He let out a sigh. "I'll be in the tunnels for most of the day, discovering all their hiding places. As soon as Dougal and Iain get back with the Wildmen we can attack."

"We must continue with the idea of small attacks in localized areas. It would not do to go against them in any large way since they outnumber us ten to one."

"They won't for long," he assured her, pulling on his trousers and boots. He ran his hand over his bearded face, realizing how long he'd been here. He hadn't shaved in nearly two months.

Aine stepped into a loose-fitting gray silk dress, buttoning it up the front. "I'll take a group of my advisors, and—" she began.

"I forbid you to do anything in your condition," Harold interrupted.

Aine swiveled to stare at him. "*You* forbid?" She laughed. "Do not forget that I am queen."

"You are close to your time, Aine. If something were to happen now—"

Her emerald eyes flashed angrily. "*You* do not tell me what I am to do, nor do you take over as though you own me! Do you understand?"

The warrior goddess stood in front of him with her hands on her hips, and she was fearsome to behold. And yes, he had to admit he was even more aroused. He bowed low and placed his hand on his heart. "I do, my queen, and it won't happen again."

She gave him a scathing look before sweeping from the room.

He followed her down the stairs and into the dining hall where several of her advisors were having breakfast. He watched her talking with them and moved on toward the stairwell that led to the tunnels. He would eat later.

Harold was deep inside the tunnel when he heard a noise. At first it was barely a scraping sound, but as he crept forward in the dark it became more pronounced. Someone was in here with him. He paused to listen and drew his sword carefully out of its scabbard. A moment later there were flying things all around him, the high-pitched screeches making him want to plug his ears. He slashed with his sword, feeling it bite into flesh, the shrieks as creatures fell. A few moments later they were gone. He crouched to examine the bodies. They were Sluagh. How they found their way into the tunnels beneath Aine's castle he had no idea, but he had to go back and warn the queen. This trip of theirs had to be a scouting trip since he was able to dispatch them so easily, but next time they would come prepared. This tunnel would need to be plugged up.

"Take Frel and Turmer and seal it off," she told him after he described what had happened. "We will need to post guards at all the tunnel exits. I do not want this to happen again."

Frel and Turmer were two of her most trusted Tel-quessir soldiers. Between the three of them they managed to destroy the tunnel exit, spending most of the day hauling rock and sweating. When Harold got back to the castle he was covered in sweat and dirt and very irritable.

"Is it completed?" she asked when he came into the throne room.

"Yes. And I've posted guards on all the other exits. I need a bath," he said, walking past her toward the door leading to the stairs and her bedchamber.

"When you've cleaned up please meet me under the castle. We have some heavy business to discuss."

Harold nodded and kept going.

When he descended the many floors to the meeting room under the castle he wasn't prepared for what he found. Seated around the table were many Fae he'd never seen before. They were ugly dwarf-like creatures that he would not want to meet under any other circumstance.

The queen turned when he entered. "These Fae have pledged to our cause," she said. "I want you to fill them in on what has been done so far and how we can employ their special magic."

Harold gazed around at the frightening faces with the red eyes. He did not like the look of them. "I'll do the best I can," he assured her, watching her rise from her chair. Her hand was on her belly and her color didn't look right. "Are you all right?" he whispered as she walked by him.

"Just a little tired." And then she was gone from the room and he heard her skirts swishing as she climbed the stairs.

He turned back to the table. "What do you bring to this war that will benefit the queen?" he asked in his Kenneth brogue.

One of them stood, his small stature a surprise. "We are very familiar with castles. You might say they are our bread and butter." He made a sound that could have been a chuckle and looked around. "We wear iron shoes and we can move very quickly. And we do like to kill."

There was a murmur of assent. "Tell us who you want killed and we will be happy to oblige, especially if there is a lot of blood involved with the killing."

Harold wasn't sure what to say to that. "The Sluagh are our enemies," he said. "They are the ones we want to drive from Otherworld."

The man looked around at his companions before facing Harold. "Do you care how it is done?"

Harold thought about that for a minute. "What exactly is your method?"

The hideous creature laughed, a grating sound as he shape shifted into a beast with razor sharp teeth. When he shifted back he pulled an iron pike from under the table. "Let's just say we thrive on blood. The queen assured us that if we did her bidding we would be paid in whatever currency we desired. Our currency is blood. Now if you want these Fae as prisoners or alive, we are not the ones you should hire."

Bile rose into Harold's throat. "Do you eat your victims?" he managed to ask.

"Sometimes," the creature answered. "It depends on how hungry we are." There was a rumble of low laughter around the table.

They killed with iron pikes or as the terrible beasts they shifted into. They ran on iron shoes, a metal that was normally anathema to faeries. What they did with their victims had to be of no concern, although the thought of it did not sit well. "The queen seems to think you can do the job for us. Now let's discuss strategies."

It was hours later that Harold released the Brags, as they called themselves, into one of the tunnels. They promised to find any members of the Sluagh who might be hanging around the exits. "If they aren't there you can try and find them, but be careful. They are many and you are few."

"Never mind about that," a particularly gnarled and ugly one said. "We are quick and they are not immune to our iron." His eyes glittered. "And we haven't had a good meal for a few days."

"Report back to the queen tomorrow," Harold told them, watching them disappear, one by one, into the tunnels. He had a very bad feeling about this, but the queen had found them, and he had to trust her judgment.

When he entered the bedchamber a short time later the queen was stretched out on the bed with her eyes closed. "Aine? Are you all right?"

Her eyes fluttered open and she turned her head. "I had some twinges and felt the need to rest. Nothing to worry about."

He sat on the bed next to her. "What kind of twinges? Could it be the beginning of labor?"

She smiled, reaching for his hand. "I am in control of things. Now stop worrying and tell me about the meeting."

"I'm concerned about their methods. They seem bloodthirsty and are obviously mercenaries—what's to keep them from turning on us?"

"They sought me out and I felt the need to employ them. If they manage to kill our enemies it will be worth it. I am not picky at this point."

"What do you know of them, Aine?"

A grimace crossed her face and she let out a small cry.

"Aine? What's happening?"

"I think it's time," she said, her forehead creased with pain.

"But it's too early—it's—"

"Please call Shree."

Shree was the older Tel-quessir faery who looked after the queen. "Is she a midwife?"

"Harold, please do as I ask!" she cried, her hands going to her belly.

But when she let out a shriek that rattled the windows he knew it was too late. He was not leaving her side. He would have to deliver this baby.

He took off his coat and rolled up his sleeves, heading into the bathroom for towels and hot water. When he came out again she was hunched over breathing hard. "Take hold of my hand and breathe with me," he said, sitting behind her and cradling her body against his. Sometime later, after Harold had stripped off her dress and was massaging her belly, she let out a scream that went on and on.

"Help me up," she ordered. When he pulled her to a sitting position she moved to the floor, crouching like an animal.

"What can I do to help?"

"Hold me around the middle. My legs might give way. The baby is coming." She grunted in pain and began to breathe rapidly. He felt the tension in her taut belly as she grunted and pushed, his own breath in rhythm with hers as he held her upright. "Keep breathing," he whispered.

It was not long after this that she gave a little cry and sagged against him. His arms strained to hold her up. And then he saw the baby's head between her legs, blood and all the rest of it coming with it. "Aine, the baby is here. I'm going to lower you to the floor so I can cut the cord and clean it up." She moaned as he moved between her raised knees, his knife cauterized and ready to cut the cord. He carefully cleaned them both up and carried Aine to the bed, placing the swaddled baby at her breast.

"It seems that Kenneth is skilled at midwifery," she whispered sometime later. After that statement she closed her eyes and fell into an exhausted sleep, the tiny baby boy resting against her.

The war was moving forward and in the past weeks the Sluagh had suffered many casualties. Harold had taken over the role of commander since the queen was still recovering from the birth. He spent hours in what he now thought of as the war room, discussing strategy and giving orders. Even with the many Wildmen and other recruits Dougal and Iain had brought to the castle, the Brags were the ones who had turned the tide.

Known also as Hobgoblins, they were ruthless and vicious, their methods ones that Harold could barely tolerate, and yet he had to give them credit.

This morning's meeting was with Dougal and ten of the most experienced men who stood with the farmer turned soldier. The room was not big enough to accommodate the many who had pledged themselves to the Fae queen.

Dougal was the first to speak, his canny gaze on Harold. "Things have turned in our favor," he said. "I am missin' home, and once this next skirmish is at an end I plan to head there. Is that to yer likin', Kenneth?"

Harold chuckled. "Glad you recognize who's in charge here--and yes, to your question. The plans are in place for tomorrow night's strike, and if it's successful you are welcome to take time for yourself."

"And you? Do you plan to stay here forever?"

Harold looked away; his thoughts were conflicted as he contemplated his separate lives. Here he was the commander and the father of a baby boy. Aine had named the baby, Beinion, Kenneth in Elven. It was an honor he had yet to thank her for. Because of how busy he was he rarely thought of Maeve and Airy. And when he did he quickly turned his thoughts elsewhere. He sighed and turned to his friend. "Once the war is over I'll go back. Until then I'm needed here."

Dougal accepted this without comment. "Let's get to the plannin' then, shall we? I am looking forward to some time with my woman."

Once the meeting was over and everything had been planned out to the tiniest detail, Harold headed up the long stairway. There was something pulling at him, something on his mind he didn't want to look at. In the past when his thoughts turned to Maeve she was always there, in his heart. Even during the months leading up to the birth of Aine's baby Maeve was with him. But now when he thought of her there was only emptiness. He didn't know if she had turned away from him, or he had turned away from her. Whatever it was he had to find out.

It was another two weeks before Harold explained to the queen that he needed to go back to Tiadan. "I have to check on Maeve and Airy." But the reason was more than that. Just this morning after he'd carefully extricated himself from Aine's arms, he'd seen Airy sitting on the floor of the bedchamber. The phantom had regarded him with sad eyes. Was this a product of his imagination caused by guilt? Whatever it was he knew he had to go back.

When he returned from another meeting with the Brags, the queen was sitting up in bed, the baby at her breast. "Have I ever given you the idea that you were to stay with me indefinitely? I've needed you these past weeks, but I'm stronger now and can manage, especially since the war seems to be going our way."

Harold gazed at the dark-haired babe in her arms. "I never said how much I appreciate the name you've given him. It means a lot to me."

Her mouth curled in a smile. "It was Kenneth who came to my rescue the day of the birth, and Kenneth who has stood beside me all these months. I would have named him Kenneth, but it must be Beinion, the elven equivalent. He is of royal blood and will be king one day. " She gazed down at the baby. "I have a sense that he will resemble you when he's older."

When she looked up again her eyes were misty. "I see that it is Harold who feels the need to go to Tiadan. Try not to become entangled in these two sides of yourself. One is warrior, father, and many other things as well, and the other—the other is Maeve's mate and the father of her child."

When Harold bent to kiss her she put her arms around his neck. "I hope you sort out any confusion about who you are, Harold. Know that no matter what side of yourself is present, you are a special man who will always be in my heart."

He straightened. "That sounds like goodbye forever. I hope you don't think that I—"

She shook her head, her eyes clouding. "I have no thoughts regarding the future. I only know that it rarely goes the way I expect it to. Take care."

He bent once more to place a kiss on top of his baby's head and then left the room.

When Harold walked out the front entrance of the castle he had tears in his eyes. He found Argyll in the meadow and pulled himself up onto the wide back. He'd long been without a saddle or bridle. He kicked the horse forward, beginning the long downhill ride toward Tiadan.

It took weeks to get to Tiadan, his attention taken by wounded soldiers heading home and men he knew who were still engaged in fighting. When they asked him what he knew, he told them that the tide had turned. "You are welcome to head home now," he told them. "The faeries we hired have pushed the enemy back. If things keep going the way they have, the war will be over in a week or two at most." But as he said the words he wondered--Hobgoblins were not trustworthy and he worried that they might continue with their efforts long after they were needed. It was the blood they wanted and the flesh that kept them from starving. Why had he ever agreed to employ them? And yet if he hadn't, these very same faeries would have been fighting against the Tel-quessir and the Gwyllion, a scenario that was even worse. He worried for Aine and the baby, the other faeries in the castle who he'd come to care about. How could he keep in touch with her? Would she send someone to fetch him if she found herself in danger?

He rode on, trying to concentrate on Maeve and Airy. They'd been alone long enough. They needed him, and if he allowed Harold to come to the fore, he could see he needed them as well.

When Harold rode into Tiadan there was a decided lack of activity, as though the town had been abandoned. But it was spring now and the weather was warm, the sun shining down from a sky filled with billowing clouds. He didn't stop to find out, pushing the big horse into a trot toward Tannith's house. On the way by he glanced at his unfinished project, surprised to see it more completed than how he'd left it. And yet it was obvious by the dark gray streaks on the fresher logs that it had been left like this for some time.

He slid off in front of Tannith's cottage and gave the horse a slap on his rump. "Go find Pooka," he said, watching him amble away.

He pushed the door open, happy to see Tannith standing in the kitchen. She turned when she heard him come in, her eyes going wide. "Ye've finally returned!" she cried, coming to give him a hug.

He looked around. "Where's Maeve?"

Tannith shook her head, her eyes welling. "She's gone, Harold, and taken your bairn with her."

Harold suppressed a gasp. "Gone where?"

Tannith shrugged. "She dinna say. All I know is she is no longer in Otherworld."

"Where did she go?"

"I'm tellin ye, Harold, she left here with narry a word, and when I called out to her she refused to turn back. The day before she told me she'd had a vision, but she wouldn't tell me what it was."

"How long ago was this?"

Tannith counted on her fingers, her eyes in the middle distance. "I would say a fortnight, maybe longer. When I heard there was fightin' goin on I half expected her back, but she never came."

"Fighting—where?"

"There are some fearsome dwarves that have decided to wreak havoc across the countryside."

Harold gazed into the distance. "I was worried about that."

"Tiadan has closed up until we can get more help. I keep myself safe with the hexes I've placed here and there around the house." She smiled. "Learned from my dear mother."

Harold had a rising fear of what he might have unleashed. He'd been right to worry. He only hoped Maeve and Airy hadn't been caught up in it. "She must have gone to Bailemuir. I certainly hope she didn't go back to the States."

"As I said, I canna tell ye. She's been very sad for a long time and I can understand why she decided the way she did." Tannith stared at him with narrowed eyes.

"You're saying this is my fault."

"You've been gone for months, Harold. Airy is near to walkin'. What did you expect her to do, wait forever? And what she told me about her visions was enough to have me fretting as well." She shook her head. "You with the queen and a wee bairn lyin' between ye." She frowned, turning away.

Harold felt a sudden sharp pain below his ribs. "I—it was Kenneth with the queen, not me."

Tannith laughed. "That is a poor way to account for your behavior, I must say. I would nay expect to get her back, especially with that as your only excuse. Now off with ye," she said, shooing him out. "Go and find her and try to come up with a better reason for what ye've been up to."

Harold gave her a wan smile and left the house, jogging into the forest to find his horse. Argyll would get no rest today.

CHAPTER THIRTY

I turned to my mother who had said something I didn't hear.

"Maeve, really. What has gotten into you? You stare at the wall and seem to be deaf."

"I told you what's wrong, mother. You of all people should understand how I feel. Harold is in love with another woman, or I should say *faery*, and they have a baby now. How would you feel?"

Finna sighed and came to sit next to me at the table. "You have always been strong, even before you became the Willow. Now tap into that strength and stop feeling sorry for yourself. You have a baby to take care of, one who is about to take her first steps."

"And Harold is not with us to see it," I muttered, trying to stop the fresh bout of tears.

"When I was younger than you I kicked your father out of my life. He's back now, but it took us twenty years to reconcile. I had you all to myself for two and a half wonderful years before he stole you away. Think how much better your life is. You have your child with you, and there is a good chance that Harold will show up here and—"

"And what—?" I interrupted, "Give me some lame excuse about what he's been doing with Aine? They have a baby together, mother—a baby! He's been gone for months! No. I've been thinking hard these past few days and I've decided things would be better for me in Milltown. At least there I can get a regular job and see regular people and maybe not think of him every second of every day." I looked down where Airy played on the floor with a set of blocks my father had made for her. She gurgled happily and looked up, her eyes meeting mine. They were the same shape and mossy color as Harold's. I smiled at her and she smiled back. "He's missed so many milestones in her life. He's such a fool."

"I felt the same way about your father, Maeve. And yet I loved him all those years, even after he kidnapped you."

"He kidnapped me for a reason, Mum. You told me it was to keep me safe from Brandubh."

"Yes, it was. But at the time it was hard for me to remember that. I was furious with him."

"What are you two talking about?" my father asked, walking into the cottage.

"You, actually," my mother replied, smiling sweetly. He came over to her and planted a kiss on the top of her head before lifting Airy into his arms and swinging her around. She let out a cry of joy.

"We certainly like having you two around," my father said, placing Airy on the floor again.

"Don't get too used to it. I'm planning to go back to the States."

My father glanced from me to my mother, a frown appearing between his thick graying brows. "When did that come about?"

"About five minutes ago when I thought about it," I said. Airy began to cry and I reached for her, pulling her into my lap to feed her. "I can't stay here forever--there's nothing for me in Bailemuir. And I don't want to live in Otherworld without Harold."

"Maybe you won't need to," my father said, glancing out the window. I looked up to see Harold's dark head moving by, and a moment later there was a knock on the door.

His hair had grown past his shoulders and he had a full beard, his eyes dark with an emotion I couldn't identify. "She's so big," he finally managed after greeting my parents.

"It's been many months," I told him coldly, looking down at where she rested against me.

"How about a cup of tea?" my mother asked in a cheery voice, bustling toward the Aga.

Harold nodded. "I'd love one. It's been a long day and I had to avoid several conflicts on the way out of Otherworld. A new terror seems to have been unleashed, and apparently I was the one who unleashed it."

I looked up. "What are you talking about?"

"The dwarves known as Brags. You must have seen them on your way here."

"No. My trip was uneventful, boring even. Maybe Pooka was able to steer clear of them."

Harold sighed and ran his fingers through his dirty hair. "They were fighting for the queen, but now that the war has pretty much come to an end they've branched out."

"They just like to fight?" I asked, watching him.

"They kill to eat. And it is human flesh they seem to like best."

"Oh, lovely," I said, my attention going to the baby who had turned to gaze at Harold. I quickly closed my dress and held the baby out. "Would you like to hold her?"

Harold looked nervous for a moment, moving out of his chair to take her from my arms. When he held her up in the air she let out a laugh, a huge smile appearing on her face. "Airy came to me," Harold said, moving her up and down. "I saw her in the castle. It's why I had to come back."

"That was your only reason?" I asked sarcastically. "Don't you have a baby up there to keep you occupied?" Out of the corner of my eye I saw my mother signal my father.

"We have some errands to run in town, Maeve. We'll be back in an hour or so," she said, taking hold of my father's arm.

I watched them leave the house before turning back to Harold. "Is it a boy or a girl?"

He looked down. "Boy. Aine named him Beinion, elven for Kenneth."

"Kenneth. So it's been Kenneth all this time? Kenneth who decided to stay with the queen, is that your excuse?"

"Maeve, I—" Harold put the baby on the floor. "I had to stay because of the war. Aine had just given birth and wasn't strong enough—"

"So the Harold/Kenneth duo came to the rescue. I get it. What I don't understand is how you could stay away as long as you did. Have you thought of us at all?" I stared at him. "Why are you here?"

"I need to make amends for what I did—I understand that. But what you said was true. It was Kenneth who stood by the queen and organized the troops and defeated the Sluagh."

"Bullshit, Harold." I got up and began to pace, my hands clenching and unclenching. I wanted to punch him. "You were gone for five full months. I went through hell wondering when you'd be back, *if* you'd be back. I didn't know if you were alive or dead until I had the visions. And the visions made things even worse. I saw you with her—saw you making love to her, and in bed with the queen, the baby too! I saw you help her through the birth! I hate you, Harold!" I picked up Airy, making her cry, and headed out the door.

I was sitting on the weathered log gazing at the ocean when Harold arrived next to me. He didn't speak, just stared toward the sea, his hands on his thighs. The baby played in the sand, her earlier irritation gone.

"I wasn't thinking clearly," he finally said. "Aine is—Aine has part of my heart, I can't deny it, but I was being honest earlier when I said it was Kenneth who cares for her. I know nothing about helping a woman through labor and yet Kenneth seemed completely capable of knowing what to do. I was Kenneth until the day I saw Airy sitting on the floor of our bedchamber."

I heard the words, *our bedchamber,* feeling sick inside. I didn't say anything, waiting for him to continue.

"As soon as I saw her, Harold reappeared, and I knew I had to go back. I'm sorry, Maeve. I know I've hurt you, but you have to admit that it was you who set it all in motion."

I turned to him. "That again? It doesn't fly anymore, Harold. Tannith and I talked about it, and I realized that you could have said no. I am no longer guilty for you being with the queen or having a baby with her, or any of the other things you'd like to put on my shoulders. You're a grown man, and if you want to see your child you'd better be honest with yourself. I'm moving back to the States and I'm taking Airy with me."

Harold stared at me. "You can't do that, Maeve."

"And why not? You have an entire other family to live with now. Why would you care?"

He grabbed me by the arm. "Because I love you."

I twisted out of his grasp. "No, you don't. If you did you wouldn't have been gone as long as you have. Why not succumb to the Kenneth part of yourself and have more babies with your precious queen? I'm done with you."

When I stood he grabbed my hand, pulling me to him. I could hear his labored breathing, smelled the sweat and the pine resin from his ride here through the forest. For one moment I softened in his arms, but when he bent to kiss me I pulled away. "No. You don't get off this easily. If you want us back you'll have to prove it." I picked up the baby and walked away from him, heading toward the small cove. The sea was like indigo glass, the sun warming my bare arms.

"Prove it, how?" he asked, running after me.

I stopped and turned. "You'll have to figure that out, won't you? Now go away and leave us alone."

I kept going, walking quickly along the shoreline. When I finally looked back he wasn't there. And then the tears came and I sagged to the sand, sobbing like my heart would break— but it was already broken.

It was close to dinner by the time my parents returned. I related the conversation, trying hard not to cry again.

"Maeve, this is a bad idea. You and Harold have been living in Otherworld for over a year; getting a job in Milltown will not be easy. You have no money, no place to stay—"

"I have my camping gear. It's stored in my VW bus."

"And who's been paying the rent on the storage garage?"

I met my father's worried gaze, realizing that my bus had probably been sold to pay off the rent. "What about your house? I could stay there."

"I sold it when I moved here."

I watched Airy playing on the floor, feeling my world crumble in on top of me. "What should I do? I have no place to live in Otherworld; Harold never finished our house. I can't stay here much longer."

"How did you and Harold leave things?" my mother asked from where she worked at the stove.

"He told me he loved me and I told him he had to prove it."

"Prove it, how?" my father asked, puzzled.

"I don't know! I was just so angry."

"Where did he go?"

"How should I know? Is Argyll still here?"

"I saw him in the meadow when we got back from town."

I shook my head, feeling like I wanted to go to bed and pull the covers up. "He's around then. I hope he's thinking about us and not about the queen. I can't stand him right now."

"Maeve, you need to give him a chance. You two have had a rough year with the baby being born and then the uprising in Otherworld. And that thing with Gan Ceanach you mentioned would have broken up most couples. His being here proves how he feels about you."

"Does it? Maybe he figures he has the queen and he can have me too. It isn't happening, Mum. I'm not going to play second fiddle to that woman."

Finna pursed her lips and turned away to begin working on dinner.

Harold didn't return that night and by nine I took the baby and went into my room. I lay awake thinking about what I'd said, wondering if I'd been too harsh. But the excuses he'd made about why he was away all those months didn't cut it. When I closed my eyes I could see him with the queen. I let out a piercing shriek and brought my mother running.

She tapped on the door. "Are you all right?"

"I'm fine, Mum."

"It doesn't sound like it, Maeve. Now try and get some sleep. I'm sure you and Harold will talk tomorrow."

When she left I lay awake remembering how we'd been before my fatal mistake—if only--but it was too late for recriminations. Harold had been sleeping with another woman, a gorgeous woman—and they had a baby together. And the hardest part for me was the vision in my mind of him helping her through the birth. Somehow that seemed like the worst betrayal of all. How could we ever get past that?

It was sometime after breakfast that Harold knocked on the door. My mother answered it and greeted him just as she always had, with a hug and a kiss. Airy was on my lap and when she saw him her face lit up. She held out her arms.

"Your baby recognizes you," Finna told him, gesturing for him to sit. "Have you had your breakfast?"

Harold shook his head, his gaze going to me. "I'm not very hungry." His eyes looked hollow, his entire demeanor somewhat defeated. "I didn't sleep well, last night," he began, looking at me. "I—"

I stood. "I don't want to hear your sob stories, Harold. Save it for the queen."

"Maeve, really!" my mother said. "There's no need for rudeness."

"Isn't there? This man left his family to shack up with the faery queen, mother—you don't think that's a reason for me to be pissed off?"

Airy gurgled and reached for him and I handed her over. "Maybe it's time you get to know your daughter again," I said, heading for the door. "If you want to talk seriously I'll be down by the ocean. But don't come to me with a bunch of stupid excuses, Harold."

An hour or so later Harold brought Airy down to the beach. He put her on the sand next to me. "I can't believe how much she's changed. She's making sounds like words now, and I swear she's going to walk any minute." He sat next to me and stared out at the sea.

"Too bad you missed all of it." I turned to look at him. "I hate to feel like this."

"Then don't," he said, his moss eyes meeting mine. "As soon as you forgive me we can move on."

"Is that your solution? Give me one good reason why I should."

"I told you already—it was Kenneth. I know you think that's a lame excuse but it's the fucking truth."

"Kenneth used to love me, or at least he said he did."

Harold grimaced. "Kenneth is easily swayed when it comes to the fairer sex."

"Oh brother. Yesterday I asked for some proof, Harold. Anything occur to you?"

"How can I prove that I love you, Maeve? I'm here now and I want to be with you. If that isn't enough then I may as well leave."

I stared at him. "I think that's a good idea."

"You want me to leave?"

"I do."

I watched him rise to his feet, his eyes dark with pain. "I'm sorry for all of it," he said. And then he turned and walked away.

I sat there for another hour trying to stop crying. Airy seemed oblivious as she played with shells and rocks. Harold and I were at an impasse unless one of us could get beyond it. But I was still so angry with him—so hurt that he'd chosen the queen over me. How could I ever trust him?

It was late afternoon when my mother told me she and my father had spoken with Harold while I was at the beach. "He told us what you said. He's hurting, Maeve. He loves you and wants to make amends."

"How can I trust him, Mum?"

"Sometimes it has to be a leap of faith. He knows how much he hurt you and feels terrible about it. He asked us to talk with you."

"How can you and Dad help with this? It's an emotional rift between us and I have no idea how to mend it."

"Harold is a good man," my father said. "He admitted he lost his way. He's terrified that you won't ever forgive him."

"I may not."

"I wish I could impress upon you how important forgiveness is. Without it we wouldn't be here now."

I stared at my father. "Am I supposed to forgive him just like that? We haven't even discussed anything yet."

"What is there to discuss?" Mum asked. "You are both guilty in your own ways, Maeve. He felt hurt by your behavior too."

"My behavior? What did I do?"

"You set the entire thing up," my father answered.

So Harold had told them all of it, trying to gain their sympathy. And it had worked. My gaze was caught by Argyll walking by. "Where did he go?"

"He went to the bar to have a beer and talk with Colum."

I thought of the bar in town and how long ago it had been since I'd had a glass of wine or listened to music. "If you could watch Airy for an hour or two I can go and get a glass of wine myself. If he's there it will give us another chance to talk."

Both my parents looked relieved. "We'd love to, Maeve," my mother said. "But I think you should change first."

I looked down at the milk stained T-shirt I was wearing, the cut off jeans that had seen better days. "If you've noticed I've been wearing the same two outfits since I've been here. Where are the rest of my clothes?"

"Look on the shelf in the closet," my mother said, reaching to pick up Airy.

In the other room I was surprised to see all the clothes I'd brought along when I came to visit my mother over a year ago. None of them were summer clothes, but I found a clean T-shirt and jeans that would work. They were looser than they'd been, and when I looked in the mirror I was shocked to see how hollow my cheeks were. I had let myself go in the past weeks not even bothering to comb out my hair. No wonder my parents were worried about me. I took the clothes and went to take a shower.

When I came out dressed in clean clothes with my hair washed and combed I saw the approval in my mother's eyes. "You look very much like your old self, Maeve. Now take the mini and go have a good time."

"You trust me to drive? I don't have a license—oh--and I have no money either."

My father pulled his wallet out and handed me forty pounds. "If you get stopped, every copper in Bailemuir will be happy to let you off. They all know the stories."

I smiled and stuffed the money in my pocket. "Airy should be fine until I get back. If she gets hungry spoon some of that porridge into her."

I parked the mini across the street from the pub and wended my way across the street. Cars whizzed by, scaring me, the raucous sound of music blaring from their radios. I felt shell-shocked by the chaos. When I entered the pub the music was even louder, screeching from speakers and mixing with the din of conversation. I saw Harold at the bar with his back to me and went to find a table. But my appearance had not gone unnoticed and before I could sit down Colum was bellowing my name. "Maeve, the Willow!" he shouted. "This woman saved a land from being overrun by a tyrant. Give her a hand!" Everyone turned to stare at me before clapping and whistling. My cheeks burned. After the clapping died down Colum came over and gave me a big hug. "Did you see Harold?" he asked, pointing toward the bar.

"I did. Can you bring me a large glass of white wine?"

He looked at me quizzically. "Don't you two have a baby?"

"Yes, a baby girl." I smiled.

Colum shrugged and headed away. When he reached the bar I saw him whisper something to Harold. A second later Harold was off his bar stool and heading my way with a beer in his hand. "What prompted you to come here?" he asked, pulling the chair around to sit in it backward. He looked me over appraisingly.

"I wanted a glass of wine."

"Now who's bullshitting?" he asked, smiling. "You knew I'd be here—don't deny it."

"Harold, I can't have this conversation right now. For one thing I can barely hear myself think," I shouted over the din.

He watched me as he took a sip. "This beer tastes better than anything I've ever had."

Colum appeared and plunked a glass down in front of me. "Anything you two need is on the house," he said, before turning back toward the bar.

"We're minor celebrities," Harold said, leaning toward me so I could hear.

His breath was sweet with the faint aura of the beer he was drinking. I picked up my glass and took my first sip. "Oh," I said, taking another sip. "This is utterly delicious!"

We shared a pub meal and had two more drinks each, our conversation veering from one subject to the next. It seemed so normal to be sitting here in a pub drinking and talking. But the buzz and clink of cutlery and the constant noise was giving me a headache. "I have to get out of here," I finally said, rising.

Harold hurried after me and when we reached the road he grabbed my arm. "Don't go back yet. I need to talk to you."

"Isn't that what we've been doing?"

"I mean serious talking—about us and the future. I've decided what to do to prove my love."

I stopped. "What?"

"I'm going to go back and finish our house—that is if you still want to live there, or want to live with me."

"And what's to keep you from heading off to the castle again? I don't trust you."

Harold looked away. "We'll have to have an agreement, Maeve. I have a baby up there and I can't just ignore that fact. If I promise to only go to see Beinion, would that satisfy you?"

I was just tipsy enough to find this funny and I began to laugh, doubling over as the irony of it all hit me. Here we were in a modern town outside a pub and Harold was talking about whether or not he was going to have sex with the queen of the faeries. "I have a feeling you won't be able to resist," I blurted out, unable to stop laughing.

"Jesus, Maeve, are you drunk?"

When I looked into his familiar hazel eyes I felt a shift, and before I registered what I was doing I'd reached up and planted a kiss on his mouth. What I'd intended to be a quick kiss turned into something very different as his arms came around me. We stood in the middle of the street, the sound of honking cars drifting away as we clung together. "Get a room!" I heard someone shout.

When I pulled out of his arms he kept hold of me. "Maybe we should take his advice," he said, his liquid gaze on mine.

"I only have forty pounds." I watched him pull out his wallet fat with bills. "Where did you get that?"

"I had it with me when I first went into Otherworld-- changed the dollars into pounds when I landed at the airport." He counted out bills. "I think we have enough."

We ended up booking a room above the bar of the pub, Colum looking us over curiously as he led the way upstairs. When Harold handed him a wad of bills he shook his head. "I meant what I said earlier—it's on the house."

I was beginning to sober up by the time we were in the room with the door closed, my heart beating erratically. Was I ready for this? "The baby—"

"Airy will be fine," Harold said, pulling my loose T-shirt over my head. He kissed me and pulled me with him to the narrow bed, both of us falling clumsily onto the quilt. I registered his urgency as he undid my jeans and pulled them down, his hands moving across my body. "I've missed you," he said, his eyes glittering.

I suddenly came to my senses and pulled back. "Really? You've had the queen to look after your physical needs."

He stopped what he was doing to stare at me. "The queen isn't you."

I laughed. "She certainly isn't—she's gorgeous for one thing, and—"

"Stop, Maeve. I am not in love with Aine. I know it'll take a while for this to sink in, but it's you I love. And you look amazing now. You've filled out since—"

"Since I tried to starve myself to death?"

Harold grimaced. "Don't remind me. When I realized you were gone from my headspace I completely freaked out."

"Gone from your…what?"

Harold pushed back to rest on his elbows. "Since we first met in college whenever I thought of you, you'd be there, in my head. It didn't matter what was going on. Even during the time I was with the queen—that is until a few weeks ago. When you weren't there anymore, I—" he turned away to wipe his eyes. "I felt so fucking alone."

I watched him for signs that this was a story to get me to have sex, but I knew in my heart it wasn't. "You know the worst thing about all of this was the vision of you delivering the baby. I could take everything else, but that—" I stared at him, my eyes filling, "that was just too much."

He watched me, his own eyes filling. "I can understand that, Maeve. I wish I'd delivered our baby, but Harold isn't capable of it."

I laughed. "That is the lamest thing I've heard you say."

"It's true. I watched myself doing things I couldn't believe. It was extremely weird." He gazed at me. "If you aren't ready—if you'd rather talk some more and get some things worked through I'm fine with it."

"I don't know whether to trust you or not. This is kind of sudden after me shouting I hate you. I don't hate you, by the way—that's the problem. I wish I could."

"You wish you could hate me?" He pulled me close. "Maybe connecting physically can break through the wall between us—not that I'm trying to force you or anything," he whispered.

"I know you aren't. I want this as much as you do. It's just that—" But instead of letting me finish my sentence his mouth moved to mine. And a moment later I couldn't even remember what I'd been about to say. Except for the one time with the 'love talker', which didn't count, it had been months for me--

since before Airy's birth. I was ravenous for him. I tried to think clearly—didn't I need to remain angry? What if he—?

But by that time he'd removed his pants and was pressed against me. I felt my need like a freight train that couldn't be stopped. He'd always had that effect on me. The music from below got louder, the crowd rowdier as the night progressed, but we were caught up in our own music, our melody more compelling than anything coming from the bar downstairs. All sounds were drowned out as we came together, our mutual passion as natural as breathing.

I woke with a start. My breasts hurt. I turned to wake Harold who was face down sleeping on top of the bedclothes. "I have to go back, Harold. I—"

He rolled over and stared up at me, his face blue in the light from the streetlamp. "What's wrong?"

I pointed to my chest. "These. They hurt."

"I have a remedy for that," he said, moving toward me.

"The baby has to be hungry. I can't let you—"

He sat up, rubbing his eyes. "That is the deepest sleep I've had in months," he said, yawning. He looked toward the dark window. "You do realize it's the middle of the night. Do your parents lock the house?"

"No. And you can sleep with me in the guest bedroom."

By the time we got back to the house I was fully awake and feeling remorse about what we'd done. I shouldn't have given in like that. But then I realized that I was the one who started it. I parked the car and opened my door. "I hope the baby is sleeping in the guest room in the crib Mum set up. If she isn't I'm going to have to find out where they stashed her."

"Are you planning to force Airy to eat? What if she isn't hungry?"

I looked over at him. "Then we'll have to go with plan B," I said, moving ahead of him around the side of the house. I heard him chuckle as I opened the front door and we slipped inside.

My parents were lying side by side in the bed against the far wall, their light snores in rhythm. I moved across the room on tiptoe to open the door that led into the guest room, Harold right on my heels. Once we were both inside I breathed out my held breath. My baby was where she was supposed to be-- sleeping peacefully in the crib.

"Plan B?" Harold whispered. "Or do you want to wake her?"

Despite the darkness I was able to see his grin.

Chapter Thirty-One

Harold woke in Maeve's bed with his head pounding. He was not used to alcohol and he had really overdone it the night before. Maeve was still asleep, and when he looked at her he felt something stir deep inside—a feeling he'd forgotten. She was truly the love of his life, or should he say the love of Harold's life? He chuckled to himself remembering the frenzied love making above the bar and what had happened once they were here. It was like old times between them, and he had the distinct impression that it had to do with being out of Otherworld. Maybe now she would forget about her crazy idea of going back to the States. He had no desire to revisit his life in Halston, although he had to admit he'd enjoyed sitting in the pub and talking with Colum and the other men. But the Highlands of Scotland was not Massachusetts.

When he glanced over at the baby she was sitting up in her crib staring at him, her fingers in her mouth. He moved from the bed and picked her up, cradling her against him. Tears came into his eyes. He'd hardly spent any time with her since…he wiped at his eyes. She needed to be changed, but where did Maeve keep whatever she used to accomplish this? He was just about to carry her into the other room when he heard Maeve's voice.

"Where are you taking her?" she asked sleepily, sitting up.

"She needs changing."

Maeve held out her arms. "Give her to me and check in the drawer behind you."

Harold handed the baby over and did what she said, finding real diapers instead of the muslin cloths they'd been using. "These are plastic, Maeve. I'm surprised you condone using them."

"They didn't have any cloth ones. These are biodegradable at least."

When Harold placed a diaper on the bed she was feeding the baby, a serene look on her face. "You don't have a headache?"

She shook her head. "I drank a bunch of water."

Harold sat on the edge of the bed, regarding her. "Do you regret what we did?"

Maeve frowned, adjusting Airy. "Should I?"

"No. I just wondered. I know it was sudden, but…"

"I'm glad it happened so long as it leads to a serious discussion. We have a lot to talk about."

Harold nodded. "Do you think being out of Otherworld had something to do with it?"

"You mean like drinking in a pub, getting drunk, and jumping each other's bones?"

Harold laughed. "I meant more like the energy there—a lot has happened to keep us apart. Both of us have slept with others, and that doesn't help with trust issues."

Maeve raised her eyebrows, shifting the baby to the other side. "I'd hardly refer to what happened with me and Gan Ceanach, as 'sleeping with others'. What's going on with you and Aine is a completely different matter. The For one thing, it's ongoing."

Harold stared out the window, noticing the dark clouds that had rolled in since the previous night. He heard the rumble of thunder in the distance. "I have no solution for that," he finally said, turning his gaze back to hers. "I told you yesterday that I would only go to see Beinion, but—"

"But I don't believe you can make that promise," Maeve finished for him. "You love her, you're physically attracted to her. How can you deprive yourself?"

"It isn't Harold who—"

"Don't start that again. You may have two sides to your personality, but I don't buy that you're two different people."

"Why not? If you remember during the war, Kenneth was very different from Harold."

Maeve let out a sigh. "True, but not different enough to say you're a split personality. It's not like when you're Kenneth, Harold is gone, or vice-versa. And as I remember from back then, you told me that both Harold and Kenneth loved me. Now I'm not so sure about that."

"You just made my point. If I'm not two distinct personalities how can one love you and the other not?"

She shook her head and pulled her T-shirt down, bending to change the baby.

There was a tentative knock on the door "Maeve?"

Maeve glanced at Harold. "Yes?"

"Would you two like some breakfast?"

"Yes, we would," she called. "Thanks. We'll be out in a few minutes."

"No hurry, dear."

Harold met Maeve's gaze. "Guess she knows we made up."

"I hope she didn't hear all the noise we made last night."

Harold wiggled his eyebrows. "You mean the squeaky bed springs and the moaning? We're lucky Airy slept through it."

"She was sleeping like a baby," Maeve said, grinning.

Harold was glad to see her happy. It had been a long time. He watched her pick up her jeans from where she'd flung them the night before, thinking lascivious thoughts as she slipped them on.

"I've made pancakes, but if you'd rather—"

"Pancakes are fine," Harold said, helping Finna ferry plates to the table. "We got in kind of late last night and I guess we slept in." His gaze went to Maeve who was trying not to laugh.

"Alex and I didn't hear a thing. We sleep so soundly. Did the baby wake up?"

"No," Maeve answered. "And I expected to feed her again."

Harold kept his gaze on his plate, afraid of what might happen if he looked at Maeve.

Finna laughed. "I guess the porridge filled her up. You'll have to keep that in mind when you want a full night's rest." She placed the plate of pancakes on the table and sat down next to Maeve. "What is going on with you two? Yesterday you seemed at loggerheads, but I think I can assume that you've patched things up?"

"In a manner of speaking," Maeve answered, forking pancake into her mouth. "We still have a lot to talk about."

"I think you should get married," Finna said calmly. "The ceremony could do wonders."

Harold choked on his pancake and had a coughing fit. He took a sip from his mug of tea and stared across the table at Maeve.

"I—we—" Maeve met Harold's gaze. "We haven't talked about that at all," she finally said. "I don't think now is the right time. We have too many issues between us."

"That's exactly why I think it's a good idea. You would not believe what wonders a good ceremony can do. I'm not talking about a minister or the usual falderal. What I'm proposing is a unique and personal giving of vows. It can be anything you want it to be. I can invite a few people, like MacCuill, and Rea, and of course your grandfather, Eron, and others we know, and we can have it down by the beach. The weather is wonderful this time of year—well, maybe not today," she said, watching raindrops spatter against the window. "Think about it—you two stopped a war together. You saved a world. You have a baby now—you've weathered the worst of times and you're still together. You never had any kind of rite to mark what has happened. It's high time, don't you think?"

"You know," Maeve said thoughtfully, "this could be exactly what we need."

Harold stared at her in puzzlement. "Aren't you the one talking about split personalities and trust issues?" he asked.

She smiled. "We get to write our own vows, Harold. That means we can say whatever we want to say to each other."

He thought of Maeve bringing up his relationship with Aine and the baby, a vision of her chasing him with a pitchfork running through his mind. "Publicly?"

"Well, yes. Isn't that what marriage vows are all about?"

"Good!" Finna said. "I'll begin the guest list. Shall we say summer solstice?"

Once breakfast was over and they were alone in the bedroom again Harold said, "Are you out of your mind? We aren't anywhere near making that kind of commitment. If we were going to marry we should have done it before Airy was born."

"What would you like to say to me, Harold? I mean in front of a bunch of people? Seriously. I think it could clear the air between us. I'm sure it won't be binding in a legal way, if that's what you're worried about."

"That isn't at all what I'm worried about." But then he thought about it—was the idea of marriage bothering him? "Well—maybe it is. It's just that marriage is something you do when you—"

"When you love someone?"

"Well, yes, but there's more to it than that. It represents something—a deep commitment."

When he looked up she was staring at him. "I mean—I don't know, Maeve. It just seems weird timing, that's all."

"I think it couldn't be better timing. It will give both of us a chance to put what we feel for each other into words. And it could clear up the other issues."

"You mean like Aine?"

"That's one of them."

"So what do I say? 'I have affection for another woman and I have a baby with her'?"

"If that's what you feel. It doesn't change what you feel for me, right?"

Harold stared into the distance. "No, actually it doesn't."

"Now all we need are some parameters. Would you like to talk about it today or wait?"

"Wow, Maeve. You seem to have come to a lot of conclusions after one night of sex."

"Is that all it was for you?"

Harold felt heat rise into his face. "No. I felt—I *feel* like I used to—like you're my soul mate." He pointed to his head. "You're there again."

"And why do you think that is?"

"How should I know? Alcohol poisoning?"

"Think, Harold. Where are we?"

"We're—we're not in Otherworld?"

"That's right. And you know what else? The Kenneth personality does not live here."

"Kenneth?" He looked at her, puzzled. And then he got it. "You're right! Kenneth only lives in Otherworld."

Maeve smiled. "And Kenneth is the one I worry about, the one who loves the queen and has a baby with her."

"So now you believe me?"

She smirked. "Judging from last night and the stuff you said, I had to rethink things. Kenneth loves her, Harold. Admit it. It doesn't matter to me as long as I have Harold all to myself."

He met her clear gaze, a long absent feeling of freedom circling through his psyche. Otherworld felt like a weight now, as though all he did was fend off one crisis after another.

Kenneth loved intrigue and war, but Harold was interested in other things, like loving Maeve and Airy, working with his hands, reading, and maybe writing. "Do you have your powers back?"

"Are you asking whether I'm bewitching you?"

Harold laughed. "I'm serious—do you?"

She smiled. "Some. But for the first time I don't really care about that. Wanting them back so badly is what drove me to hand you over to the queen. Remember what she said about you and the baby—how she envied what I had? Not in those exact words, but it's what she meant."

"What are you saying? Do you want me to finish our house? Do you want to live here in Bailemuir? What do you want?"

"I want you and Airy, Harold. It's as simple as that. Wherever we decide to live is fine, as long as you're mine and mine alone."

"Maybe Otherworld won't work for us—is that what you're saying?"

"You're the one saying that, not me. If you think what I want won't work there, then we have to come up with another plan."

"There's a lot of nasty crap brewing in Otherworld. If the Fae dwarves keep going—"

"Do you want to fix it? Do you think you can? From how you described them they're vicious and without conscience. The queen hired them, let the queen deal with it. She has many soldiers at her disposal now."

Harold stared at her in surprise. This was a new side to her he'd never seen before. She was always out in the forefront trying to combat evil, trying to help the good guys. Maeve was a warrior and he'd seen her when all she cared about was getting rid of Brandubh and saving the people of Otherworld. Was she saying she didn't care about any of that anymore? His headache was back and this time slivers of pain stabbed into his temples. "I can't talk anymore," he said, grabbing his head. "I may have to go down to the pub and have a little hair of the dog."

"You better wait a while," Maeve said, pointing to the window. A flash of lightning zigzagged down, a crack of thunder following a second later.

He heard the rain pounding against the glass and watched it run down in uneven rivulets. He sagged back against the pillow and closed his eyes.

CHAPTER THIRTY-TWO

Once the storm moved through, Harold took the mini and left for the pub. He'd been completely incommunicado after our conversation, and I wondered whether it was what we'd talked about that had given him such a headache. He was right about me. I had no idea why, but something had changed. Maybe it was the normalcy of being out of Otherworld where I was always waiting for the other shoe to drop, or maybe it was because Harold and I had finally connected again. I'd believed him when he professed his love for me the night before. And Kenneth being swayed by the fairer sex sounded about right for a man who'd lived over a thousand years in the past. It was time to let Kenneth go.

"Do you want to talk about it?" my mother asked when I was making a cup of tea.

I turned from the Aga. "For insisting that you aren't psychic, you certainly have an uncanny way of knowing when something's on my mind."

Finna smiled. "I know you, that's all. You've never been able to hide your moods."

I brought my mug to the table and sat down across from her. "Harold and I talked, but I have no idea what's going on in his head. He seemed to accept the idea of our vows, but he's also very much involved in Otherworld."

"And how do you feel about it?"

"Honestly? The idea of staying out of the constant problems sounds good to me right now. I don't know if I'll always feel like this, but—" I looked up and met her gray-green gaze. "I want some normalcy, I guess. I have no idea what our life might be like out here, but I'm sick of the constant worry. These last few months have been nearly as enervating as the entire war! And Harold's connection with the faery queen isn't going to stop. They have a baby together."

"Does he love her?"

I shrugged. "He says he has affection for her, but insists it's only the Kenneth personality who feels that way. I don't know whether to believe him."

"I tend to wonder about that, myself. Now tell me, do you think you two could make a life here in Bailemuir?"

"I have no idea. I think Harold thrives on the adrenaline he gets from the stuff that comes up in Otherworld, but if we were here he could come and go, I suppose."

"Except you'd worry that he was going to the faery queen."

"You're right—I would. What do you suggest?"

Finna shook her head. "I'll talk it over with your father. Perhaps he'll have another perspective. Now, as to the wedding—maybe it isn't such a good idea."

"I actually thought it might help us. If we write what's in our hearts maybe we can get past all this emotional baggage. I know he loves me."

"Are you willing to share him, Maeve?"

"No. Maybe if I were a more secure person, I could, but—"

"You are not insecure, Maeve. You have done so many brave things and nearly died in the process. Give yourself some credit. What if you gave him an ultimatum?"

"You mean like, 'if you sleep with the faery queen I'll take Airy away and you'll never see either of us again'?"

"Something along those lines. What would he say?"

"So far he's tried to make a promise to only go there to see his son."

"Son? Oh my goodness—a boy. This complicates things." Her dark eyebrows knitted together as she stared into space. "What is his name?"

"He's called Beinion, elven for Kenneth. What do you mean about 'complicates things'?"

"Harold will live vicariously through him and want to teach him all he knows. He will want to be a part of his life. Believe me, if the queen had given birth to a girl she could raise her without his interference. Maybe you should try for another baby."

I gaped at her. "You can't be serious!"

"I am, Maeve. If you want to keep Harold by your side you need to give birth to a boy."

"But even if I had a boy that doesn't mean this other one doesn't exist. Harold will always be connected to Aine through Beinion."

"That is true, but if you have another baby with him he won't want to stray for long. I know this sounds rather conniving, but I think you should consider it."

"It sounds terrible, Mother. I can't believe you're suggesting it! I feel like one of those women who gets pregnant to keep her man."

"You already have your man, Maeve, this just assures that he'll stay devoted."

"But how do you make sure it's a boy?"

Finna smiled. "I will tell you exactly how to manage it."

"My god, Mum, you're like some evil witch!"

"I know some things, Maeve, things I've never shared with you. But if you are planning on taking my advice what you need to do is wait until you are ovulating to have sex. And make sure he…"

I put up my hand. "No more! I can't discuss my sex life with my mother!"

Finna shrugged and stood up. "The other things I have to tell you are not about how deep his penetration needs to be, it's about the pH of the…."

"Mum!"

She threw up her hands. "Okay, okay. I'll leave it there."

My father came into the room, glancing from my shocked expression to Finna, who seemed to radiate with some witch-like fire. "Is your mother revealing her secrets?" he asked, smiling.

"Too many," I said, standing. "I'm going to walk into town to clear my head."

"Take the trail at the top of the hill, dear. It's shorter and much more pleasant. But don't forget an umbrella. It will rain again this afternoon."

I opened my mouth in surprise. My mother was suddenly clairvoyant? I realized I did not know her nearly as well as I thought I did. But then I looked out the widow and saw clouds forming in the distance—a completely normal reason to suggest I take an umbrella along. And as to worrying about her being a witch, so far all she'd told me about assuring that we had a boy, I could have looked up on the Internet--if I even remembered how to use a computer anymore.

"So your mum thinks we should have another baby so that I'll hang around home?"

I sat next to him at the bar where he nursed a beer. Luckily we were the only ones there at the moment, all the other patrons sitting at tables scattered around the room. "A baby *boy*, Harold. That's the important part. And to have it work I suppose I shouldn't have shared it with you."

Harold let out a laugh. "Yeah, I guess the element of surprise would be better in this case. Why did you tell me?"

"Because it's ludicrous and I can't believe she suggested it? And you're my best friend. I would never deceive you like that."

He turned to stare at me. "God, I love you," he whispered.

"I love you too," I whispered back, gazing into his liquid eyes. Even though I'd shared my mother's plan, I wondered— would it work? Did I want another baby now? Airy was already a handful and she would become more of one as time went on. But then I saw the baby in my mind, hair the color of Harold's and hazel eyes just like his. He watched me from someplace in the ether. I gasped in surprise.

"What is it?"

"I think I just saw him."

Who?"

"Our baby boy." I swiveled on the stool to face him. "He looked just like you, Harold, and I think he wants to be born."

Harold regarded me thoughtfully. "We could have fun trying," he finally said, grinning.

"And maybe Harold could learn how to deliver a baby," I said.

He stared at me. "I'm sure he could."

It was mid-May when Harold announced he had to go Otherworld. "I have to see what's happening, Maeve. It's been almost two months."

"Harold, no!" The last months had been filled with plans for our 'wedding', the invitations written and sent. Somehow my mother knew how to get messages into Otherworld, something I'd never quite discovered, since there was no mail service there. We'd spent hours discussing what had happened between us, including the visions I couldn't get out of my mind, vowing to love each other no matter what obstacles were thrown at us. I stared at him in disbelief.

"Those are my friends in there. And I can't stop thinking about them."

"We're about to get married, and we've just re-established our relationship. I don't want you to go; the timing is really bad."

He frowned "The timing is always bad, Maeve. I can't stop the feelings I'm having. I know I'm needed and I can't just ignore it."

I stared out the window before turning to him again. "What about the queen? What will you do if she wants you again? I can't stand the idea of you two together. This time it will be the end of us."

Harold shook his head. "I'm not going for the queen. I'm going for my friends. I promise that even if she wants me, I'll say no; I mean it, Maeve. I can't lose you."

I watched his eyes for signs of lying, but all I saw was his mossy gaze and the tears that welled. "Okay, as long as you come back to me. Our celebration is set for June twenty-first."

He donned his homespun trousers hanging in the closet and pulled on the heavy boots. The loose-fitting indigo tunic was next, followed by his sword, which completed his Otherworld garb. "I've gotten used to indoor plumbing and having the computer at my fingertips. It'll be interesting to see how I feel about the more rustic elements."

"And how you feel about the queen," I added.

He grimaced. "I'll go for Beinion, nothing more."

"I hope so. I meant what I said."

He met my gaze. "I promise."

I carried Airy as I followed him out of our shared bedroom and through the front door. My parents had gone to town, saving him the stress of saying goodbye and listening to their protests to keep him here. Argyll waited, already tacked up with the new saddle and bridle he'd purchased at the local tack and feed store. He kissed me hard on the mouth before he mounted and turned in the saddle. "Don't let her walk until I get back."

I laughed. "Time waits for no one, Harold. Make sure you get back before she does."

I watched him ride up the ridge and disappear over the other side, hoping against hope that he would be true to his word. The idea of losing him to the queen again made me feel sick inside. But trying to keep him here when he felt the pull of Otherworld would only make matters worse. I had to trust him.

I was inside spooning porridge into Airy's mouth when my parents arrived home. My mother brought in her packages, placing them on the small counter while my father headed off to the bathroom. "Where's Harold?"

"He went to Otherworld, said he had to see what was happening."

My mother pressed her lips together. "That was sudden. Why?"

"He says they need him and I'm sure they do."

Finna let out an exasperated sigh. "They need Kenneth, you mean, the one who can fight and kill without remorse. I certainly hope he gets back in time for the ceremony."

I stared at her, surprised by the vehemence in her voice. "He will. He promised."

She turned from where she was unloading a fresh loaf of bread and several bags of vegetables. "You trust him?"

"I do. If I didn't I wouldn't be planning this so-called wedding."

"Have you taken my advice?"

"I guess you mean the baby thing. I have to wean Airy or it won't work."

"And are you?"

"I've started—it's not easy, you know."

"The more regular food she eats the less she'll need breast milk. It's as simple as that. And she's certainly old enough. Now, about the other matter—I have a few things to share that will help it along."

"More about pH and stuff like that? I've looked on the Internet, Mum, and found a lot of information." I knew now that the best positions for conceiving a boy were either doggy style, or standing up, or the woman straddling the man. And I didn't want to discuss this with her.

She smiled, reaching to place a can on a high shelf. "So you *have* been considering it." She came to the table and sat down next to me. "No. What I have to tell you is more what you might call witchy magic stuff."

I waited, intrigued for once.

"You must imagine your baby—see him in your mind and ask him to come. Name him before he's conceived and think of him while you and Harold—"

"Gotcha."

She looked up from where she'd been staring at the table with a glazed expression. "What you will need is a bit of Harold's hair. Place it and some of your own saliva in an egg-shaped box, could be part of an egg carton if you wish, and place it beneath your bed."

"Yuck!"

"That isn't so bad—you should hear the recipes for fertility."

I sighed. "It's too soon for anything yet. Airy has to be weaned, Harold has to come back—" I looked up when my father appeared and sauntered toward us.

"I take it Harold has left us?"

I nodded. "I'm sure he wants to check on the Brags. And there is his son..." my voice faded off as I contemplated this.

My father frowned. "That should never have happened," he muttered. "What I want for you two is a life full of joy without the stresses of Otherworld. Do you know how bad you looked when you arrived here? I was very worried about you. Now you have the roses back in your cheeks, and your eyes have the light in them that I remember."

"Dad, you are such a romantic." His words took my mind into the past. Before I knew anything about Finna, my father had stolen my mother's self-portrait right out of the gallery where I worked in Milltown. Drunk at the time he'd nearly been arrested. But at least it led him to tell me about my childhood. Before that I'd thought my mother was dead. I'd been angry with him for several months after that—until I found out why he'd done what he'd done.

He shrugged. "Maybe I am, but it's what got me here." He turned to Finna. "Your mother and I, we—"

"Don't bore her with our life, Alex." She reached to take Airy from my lap, holding her for a moment before placing my plump and sturdy little girl on the floor. "She's ready to be weaned, Maeve. And if I'm not mistaken she'll be walking any day now," she added, watching Airy grab hold of the table leg and try to pull herself up. She slipped back and landed on her bottom, but it didn't faze her.

"I hope Harold gets back in time to see it," I murmured, my eyes on our child. If Harold got himself killed I would never forgive him.

Chapter Thirty-Three

"**I**'m telling you, Harold, they are out of control! 'Tis a plague and no one is immune!"

Harold frowned, hoping to hell his friend was exaggerating. "What can I do?"

"I dinna know what *you* can do, but Kenneth would come in handy. That sword you're wearin' would deter 'em a bit."

Harold let out an exasperated sigh. "I'm only one man, Dougal."

"You're one man who can raise an army. Ye have a gift for it, whether you realize it or not."

"How much damage have they done?"

"They've come through here and killed at least twenty men and women. Luckily Tannith ran away into the woods or she'd be lying in a grave with the rest of 'em. Her charms only go so far. A few of our own disappeared afterward, including women and children. MacCuill has called a meeting of all the tribes to discuss it. You came back just in time."

"When is it?"

"Tomorrow—ye must have had a sixth sense."

The meeting was held at the druid castle where MacCuill had been put in charge. He was the elder now, and as such he had complete authority. The enormous table was filled with familiar faces of Wildmen Harold had fought next to, as well as Crion, Villagers and a few of the ogre-like Oillteil, who had remained in Otherworld after the end of the last war.

Everyone was talking at once until MacCuill held up his hand. "All will have a chance to express his or her views, but there will be order! We need a plan of action and I expect that when this meeting is over we will have accomplished our goal. There is not one moment to lose." He turned to Harold. "Where is Maeve?"

"I left her in Bailemuir with her parents. You do remember we have a baby?"

"That would never stop her if she had her magic back—does she?"

"She tells me she has visions from time to time. As far as moving through the ether and the rest of it, I don't know."

MacCuill sighed and turned back to the assembled crowd. "We will need to form killing groups. It isn't my way, but in order to stop these devils they must be eliminated. There is no reasoning with their kind, and driving them from Otherworld is an impossibility."

"Why is that?" a Wildman asked, his hands spread in a gesture of confusion.

"If we were able to chase them out they would only come back. They will stay until every last man, woman, and child from every species lies dead. Believe me, I've dealt with their kind before."

"We need to divide up our forces and hit them at night," a male Oillteil said, picking up the heavy club lying by his side. "I can summon more of my tribe. Just tell me where to go."

Harold recognized him as Oak, one of Maeve's first recruits during the past war. The man was strong as an ox with a caring heart, a combination not normally present in most members of this tribe. Harold turned back to the table, his gaze scanning the many men and women assembled here. They were all good people and would do their very best. "I'll lead the villagers from Tiadan," he said.

Dougal shook his head. "There are nay enough of us. We must combine forces with other villages."

"Fine, then. Just tell me where to go."

The rest of the meeting went on like this until everyone had been divided into groups. Each group had a separate part of Otherworld to patrol. Once they all had their orders the meeting broke up.

MacCuill waited until everyone left before walking out with Harold. The druid put his hand on Harold's shoulder. "I wouldn't ask this unless I thought it was imperative for our success, Harold, but I want you to ride to Baelimuir and enlist Maeve's help."

Harold gazed at the old druid, trying to think of what to say. In the end he only nodded, heading away from the castle to find Dougal.

"He wants me to bring Maeve into this," he told his friend a few minutes later. "And I'm not willing to risk her life."

"What about the faery queen? How is she faring? Does she have a strong enough force to help us go against them?"

"The Brags were fighting for her, so I don't know. I suppose I'll have to find out."

Dougal nodded. "I'll meet you in Tiadan with as many men as I can muster. Be careful—those shifting beasts can appear out of nowhere."

Harold did not look forward to seeing the queen. It had been some time and he worried that his resolve might not hold up. She held a certain sway over him that he couldn't deny. And now that Kenneth had been called on he was loath to test it. He mounted Argyll and headed out, determined to resist her, but he was sure that seeing his baby son would also have a strong effect on him. He held Maeve's image in his mind as he headed west toward the Gualan Range.

It took nearly four days of hard riding to reach the castle. He'd seen the Hobgoblins several times and had to skirt around them, going miles out of his way. Argyll was footsore and irritable by the time they reached the meadow that lay to the south of the castle. Harold dismounted and pulled off the saddle and bridle. "Rest, Argyll, and eat some of the sweet grass growing here. It will be a day or two before we head back down."

The horse regarded him solemnly and lowered his head to graze.

When Harold rapped, a burly soldier wearing leather armor opened the heavy door. "Who might you be?" he asked gruffly.

"Please tell the queen that Harold is here."

The man looked him over suspiciously and ushered him inside. "Wait here."

A few minutes later he returned. "The queen will see you now," he said, leading the way toward the throne room. He opened the door and went ahead, bowing low before ushering Harold inside.

The queen was sitting on her throne holding the baby, her emerald eyes colder than he remembered. "Harold, how nice of you to come," she said, gesturing him forward. She looked over his shoulder, "You may go, Henner," she said.

Harold heard his footsteps and the sound of the door being closed as he moved up the wide steps. He paused at her feet, bending down to show his respect. "I am here because of the dwarves, my queen. The ones who call themselves Brags."

She gestured for him to stand. "Is that the only reason?" she asked, holding out the bundle in her arms.

Harold took the baby, surprised to see how much he'd grown. When the dark eyes met his, his heart felt squeezed. He pressed the baby to his chest and closed his eyes, breathing in his scent and trying not to cry.

"He is handsome, is he not? And looks more like you every day."

"I've missed him--and you," he added, his eyes meeting hers.

"My dear, Harold, I can see the hesitation in your eyes. Do not be afraid of me. I will not bewitch you or try to take you to my bed. In your absence I have found another lover."

Harold started, feeling Kenneth rise within him. A tendril of jealousy wound through him. This was not a scenario he had anticipated. "Who is he?"

Aine laughed. "You are jealous and yet you have re-committed to Maeve. It is of no consequence. Perhaps he met you at the door?"

"The soldier who answered the door is your lover?"

"You disapprove?"

Harold thought of him again, the dark eyes and high cheekbones that made his face handsome. He had a roughness to him, but he was not an ugly man. He imagined them together and had to push the image from his mind. "I find that I'm jealous of him, my queen."

"And yet you came here with the plan to avoid my bed."

The baby made a mewling sound and he handed him back, watching the queen pull the shoulder of her dress down to expose one breast. He looked away.

"So, tell me, Harold. Why exactly did you come?"

He turned back to her. "As I said, I came because of the dwarves. They are on a killing spree. I hoped you might have a force of your own to go against them."

"They have done nothing to cause me to go against them. I have not seen them since a few weeks after you left. Why would I go after the Fae, especially since they were instrumental in stopping the Sluagh?"

"Because they are killing humans."

"And what is the human race to me? I have no desire to become embroiled in the petty wars of humans. I told you to stay out of it, and now you are paying the price."

"If I hadn't helped your castle would be rubble and all here would be dead."

She scoffed, her hand going to the baby's soft head that rested against her. "You do not know what the outcome might have been, Harold. I appreciated your help, but that does not mean that I, or my forces, must now come to your rescue. My people are safe from them and I am not willing to jeopardize the mutual agreement that we made."

"So what happens as a result of these odious creatures means nothing to you? I'd always thought you were kind, Aine, a queen who cared about others."

Her eyes narrowed. "You abandoned me and now you come here demanding my help?" When her shrill voice startled the baby, she softened her tone. "The Fae kingdom includes all faery species, not just mine or those who are under my rule. We have always kept to ourselves and will do so again. Humans are no longer welcome here."

Harold bowed and stepped off the dais. "Then I will take my leave," he said, backing away angrily.

"The one exception is you, Harold. I expect you to return from time to time to see your child," she said, sweetly. "Whether or not we are lovers has no bearing on your relationship with Beinion."

Harold nodded and turned to head out the door. In the other room the soldier met his gaze. "I am the queen's consort now. She has no use of you. I would suggest you steer clear."

"And yet I fathered her child," Harold responded with more vehemence than he'd intended. "I will come to see my son whenever I damn well please."

Outside the castle he had to stop and bend over for a moment, his anger nearly blinding him for a moment. The queen was a selfish bitch and cared nothing for anyone but the Fae. Why hadn't he noticed this before? *Because you were besotted*—a voice in his mind supplied. But it was more than that, he realized. Despite her telling him he was free to go, his long absence had hurt her deeply. There was a part of her that loved him and felt betrayed. *Hell hath no fury like a woman scorned,* he thought to himself.

CHAPTER THIRTY-FOUR

I examined the calendar on the wall, my stomach clenching with nerves. Harold should be back by now. "I think we should cancel the wedding."

"He'll be back in time," my mother answered, turning from the table where she sorted laundry.

"It's only two weeks away! He's been gone for a month. What could have happened?" I thought of the vision I'd had a week before: Harold riding through a dark forest on Argyll, his hand on his sword. The look on his face was fierce and I recognized Kenneth's rugged features. He had on leather armor and his hair was longer and tied back. The thought of something happening to him terrified me.

"The dwarves are what's happened. That's why he went. Perhaps it's taking longer than expected to get rid of them."

I thought about the queen—the baby. I'd had no visions of Harold with Aine; at least that was a good thing. "If he isn't back by the fifteenth I'm calling it off."

Finna folded a baby blanket and placed it on the table with the rest of Airy's clothes. "How is the weaning coming?"

I picked up another blanket and folded it, adding it to the pile. "Have you seen me feeding her lately? I only do it at night now."

"You seem touchy about it. Why?"

"Because I was only doing it so we could make a baby, and now—" I sat down and put my head in my hands. "And now I'm scared he won't be back."

Finna placed her hand on my shoulder. "He'll be back, Maeve. I know he will."

The fifteenth came and went with no sign of Harold, but my mother refused to let me call things off. "He will be here in time," she intoned, her eyes glazed.

My worry kept me up at night, that and my baby who wasn't quite used to sleeping all the way through the night. Several times I'd succumbed to her demands, letting her breast-feed instead of listening to her woeful crying. The closeness I felt when I fed her made up for some of my worry and loneliness. What if he never came back? What if he'd decided to stay with the queen? I'd had no more visions of him and it worried me. If Kenneth took over would Harold be strong enough to keep his promise to me?

I went about my days in a fog, trying not to think of Harold as I helped my mother with cooking, cleaning and doing the wash. Thank goodness she had a washing machine

now. The lack of a drier was only a problem when it rained--
otherwise we hung the clothes on the line.

My father had built himself a workshop and spent most of
the day there working on his furniture projects. He'd made a
small dresser for Airy, and my mother and I finished it off by
painting rabbits and flowers and other decorative designs along
the drawers and the top. Now, if only I had a house to put it in.
I thought of my unfinished house in Otherworld, longing
settling into my stomach. It was the first time I'd felt an
inclination to go back. But then I remembered the queen and
the baby. The Kenneth/Harold duo was probably rushing
around right now, doing his worst with that damn sword. No. I
wanted some peace in my life.

Pooka followed me around like a dog, and a couple of
times I'd hopped on with Airy, giving her taste of what being
on horseback was like. She loved it, as I knew she would. My
baby girl had taken her first steps without Harold there to
witness it.

It was the morning of the twentieth that I heard a nicker
from Pooka, and then an answering neigh. When I opened the
door I saw Argyll ambling down the hill with Harold on his
back. I flew from the house without stopping to put on shoes.
By the time I reached Argyll, Harold was off his back, his arms
held wide. I flung myself into them. "Where have you been?"
And then I noticed the deep cuts across his cheek, the hollow
look in his eyes, the limp that made him sway while he held me.
His long hair was filthy and filled with sticks and moss and he
stunk like sweat and dirty clothes.

"It's a long story," he said, glancing up as my mother came toward us. "I'll tell you all about it when we're alone."

When we reached the house Harold went straight to the crib, waking up Airy to plant several kisses on her baby head. She cooed and laughed, her grubby fist waving in the air. And when he put her on the floor and she walked, his eyes widened. "When did that happen?"

"Nearly a month ago, Harold. I tried to get her to hold out, but she wouldn't."

He chuckled, watching her toddle over to the table. "I wish I'd been here." And then his eyes met mine. "But I'm glad to be alive to see her now."

"You need to take a shower before dinner," I said, holding my nose.

He laughed. "Haven't had one since I've been gone. I guess I must be a bit ripe by now."

"That's one way of putting it." I went to the dresser and pulled out clean jeans and a shirt. "Clean clothes. I think we might have to burn the ones you're wearing."

During dinner Harold filled us in on how they'd managed to drive the dwarves out of Otherworld. "Kenneth came in handy," he said, glancing at me. "That sword is a godsend."

"Everything good then?" Alex asked, taking another bite of chicken.

"Not perfect by any means. Some slipped away and are surely hiding out. But at least many are dead now. I tell you the entire thing was a f---." He stopped himself in mid-sentence, looking abashed. "It was a bloody mess," he finished, his eyes meeting mine.

"What about Gan Ceanach—did you see him? Is he dead?"

Harold pressed his lips together. "He must have gone before I got there. I never saw him."

There was a silence as we all concentrated on our food. Finally I looked up. "Do you still want to go through with the ceremony?"

He grinned. "Hell, yes. I can't wait."

I smiled and grabbed his hand.

"Didn't I tell you he'd be here, Maeve?" my mother said calmly before turning to my father. "We'll keep Airy out here with us tonight. That way you two can catch up and get some real rest."

"Thanks, Mum. We do have a lot to talk about." When I glanced toward Harold he raised his eyebrows, trying to keep from laughing.

After we cleaned up Harold carried the crib out of our room and placed it close to their bed. "Are you sure you don't mind?" he asked Finna.

"Maeve's been weaning her, Harold, in preparation for—"

"Mum!"

My mother gazed at me blandly. "Well, in any case she's easy now and loves her porridge and fruit."

"How did you get the limp? And what happened to your cheek?" I asked as soon as we were in the bedroom with the door closed. I ran my fingers lightly across his recently clean-shaven face, tracing what looked like scratches from some beast.

"I shaved to get a better look at it," he said, putting his hand over mine. "It isn't as bad as I thought. The dwarves ambushed me, and if it hadn't been for Dougal, I'd be dead.

When they shift they have claws, and I guess one of them raked them across my cheek when I was falling. I hardly felt it since my leg got caught in one of the traps they set, and—"

"They set traps—like animal traps?"

Harold nodded, his eyes going dark. "I had to remove bodies from those traps so we could bury them. The people had been partially eaten and completely drained of blood. Those creatures are pure evil."

I nearly gagged, imagining it. "How many people were lost?"

"Hundreds, maybe more. I lost count."

"I'm glad I wasn't there," I muttered. "Show me your leg."

When Harold removed his jeans I saw a deep and infected wound running around the biggest part of his right calf. The teeth of the trap had dug into his flesh making holes that had not healed. "Why didn't you find a healer?"

"There was no time."

"Get up on the bed," I ordered. I placed my hands around his leg, feeling the heat from the wounds, the stench of putrid flesh wafting up. I closed my eyes and concentrated on pulling out the infection. I hadn't done this for a long time and I didn't know if I still could.

It was a long while before I heard Harold sigh. I opened my eyes, noticing that the oozing, puss-filled flesh had lessened, but it would take several more sessions to heal it completely. I needed comfrey and yarrow, two herbs my mother stocked. He was lucky his bone was intact. I finally sat back and took my hands away.

"I see you have your healing abilities back."

I shrugged and looked up. "Tomorrow I'll treat you with herbs to draw out the rest of it. That leg was festering to the point of gangrene. I can't believe you could even walk."

"I couldn't for a while, but then I decided that if I didn't, I'd end up dying of other wounds."

"What other wounds?"

He pulled off his shirt to reveal heavy purple bruising all across his ribs. I felt for any breaks or cracks. "When did this happen?"

"Early on. I took a beating when the shifters pulled me off Argyll. Something took their attention or they would have beaten me to death."

"You could have died from internal bleeding." I met his dark eyes. "And they know you—you were in charge at the castle."

"Not all of them, and these were ones I'd never seen before." He winced when I pressed against his rib.

"This one could be cracked or broken." When I moved closer to feel along the bone Harold took hold of my wrist and pulled me toward him.

He reached for my T-shirt and tugged it over my head and ran his hand along the waistband of my jeans. "Take those off."

I did what he asked, our eyes locked together. When he kissed me I forgot all about his ribs, his bruising, his leg wound or anything else. He let out one cry of pain as he rolled me on top of him, and that was the last sound I heard from him other than his panting breath and a couple of low groans that were definitely not related to pain. It didn't escape me that the position we were in was one recommended by the articles on the Internet.

"Tell me about the queen," I asked later, turning on the lamp.

Harold pushed himself up to sitting and leaned back against the pillow. "What do you want to know?"

"Did you—I mean—?"

"Did we have sex? The answer is an emphatic no. I spent a few minutes with baby Beinion and Aine. All we did was talk."

I waited for him to continue.

He turned to me with a look that seemed between anger and disbelief. "She was without sympathy about what the dwarves were doing to the humans—told me she was still on good terms with them. She said it was my fault for interfering. And she's found another lover. I met the brutish dude and we nearly got into a fist fight."

"Over her?"

"No, Maeve. I'm over the queen. This was about me, and my relationship to the queen's child. He was disrespectful. I told him I'd come to see Beinion whenever I damn well pleased."

"He implied that you shouldn't?"

"He told me he's the queen's consort now and to basically go fuck myself."

I tried to imagine this scene. "How often do you plan to see Beinion?"

Harold shook his head dismissively. "Don't we have vows to say tomorrow? I need to write mine so I don't end up red-faced and embarrassed in front of our guests."

Harold and I worked on our vows for an hour or so before he pulled me to him again. "If we're going to make a baby we need to get on it," he whispered.

"You want another baby?"

"Didn't we talk about this before I left?"

"Yes, but things have changed. I'm not worried anymore about the queen—I trust you now."

"The baby was only to keep me from falling for Aine again?"

"Not exactly, but it had something to do with it. Mum was the one who suggested it."

Harold frowned. "I have to tell you that Kenneth was alive and well as soon as I was with the queen. I tried to keep control of things, but he's strong, Maeve."

"So you barely kept from sleeping with her—is that what you're saying?"

"All I'm saying is Kenneth was jealous of her lover."

I stared at him. "There is no way I'm letting you back in Otherworld. If you go to the queen's castle to see Beinion I'm coming with you."

Harold let out a relieved sigh. "I would appreciate that, Maeve. I can't stay away, but I can't be overcome by that part of me. She has a new lover, but who knows what might happen? She was obviously hurt by my absence, not a good scenario when it comes to a warrior and ardent lover who lived in the eight-hundreds."

I laughed. "I'll take care of you, my sweet. No more Kenneth and I mean it."

He smirked. "Does anybody have a peanut?"

We both giggled and then laughed hysterically for a good five minutes.

After we'd gotten control of ourselves he turned to me. "You aren't on birth control now, are you?"

"No, and I don't plan to be. Airy's still breast-feeding, just not very much. You're serious about a baby?"

He grinned. "Let's leave it up to fate, shall we?"

CHAPTER THIRTY-FIVE

The next morning dawned with wispy high clouds, a pale blue sky indicating the beautiful day to come. Harold and I woke at the same time, our gaze meeting across the scattered bedclothes. "Gods, I'm glad to be here with you. A couple of times I wasn't sure I'd make it."

"You know what's odd? I hardly had any visions of you. I kept trying but nothing happened."

"I didn't tell you, but MacCuill wanted me to ride back here and enlist your help."

"He wanted me in Otherworld?"

Harold nodded. "He specifically asked if you had your powers back."

"So what did you tell him?"

"I didn't tell him anything. I just ignored it. I tried to keep you firmly in my mind during the entire time I was there, but I made sure I was seeing you here in Bailemuir, not in Otherworld."

"You think that's the reason I didn't have visions?"

He shrugged. "Could be. The thought of you in danger–" he shook his head. "I don't want you to ever be in danger again, Maeve. Seeing you so thin and—" He stared at me, his eyes filling.

I leaned forward and kissed him, lingering when he pulled me closer. "It's odd to imagine no conflicts, no evil faeries, no worry about bewitched ravens or homicidal dwarves. Won't our lives be kind of boring?"

Harold pulled back to gaze at me. "I have a hard time imagining being bored around you. Wherever we end up I'm sure you'll find some kind of mess to get us into."

I laughed. "Do you realize that your Kenneth side will never live outside Otherworld?"

Harold stared at me. "I hadn't thought about it, but you're right. He only exists there."

I nodded. "That means I can be sure that Harold won't run off and do anything stupid."

Harold smirked. "But won't you miss his humor and the way he makes love to you? You said you enjoyed him."

I shook my head. "That was then and this is now. No. I prefer Harold to Kenneth any day."

When he reached for me I pulled away. "We don't have time for that now. It's getting late and we both have things to do. I can't let my mother make all the food and set up the tables and all that." I heard Airy babbling in the other room, my mother and father talking in low tones.

"Crap!" he said, jumping up.

"What?"

"I have things to do too." He hurriedly pulled on his jeans.

After he left the room I gave my tangled hair a brushing. By the time I arrived in the kitchen there was no sign of him. My mother was at the table feeding Airy and looked up when I came in. "Where's Harold?" I asked.

"He and your father took off in the mini—I have no idea where they were going."

I took the spoon out of her hand. "Let me do that. You haven't even changed out of your nightclothes."

"I do have a full plate today," she said, moving toward the bathroom and the closet she'd added next to it. "Guests should be arriving by late this afternoon."

I had a twinge of nerves. "What am I going to wear?"

"That sweet summer dress that's been hanging in your closet since you left for Otherworld—it's perfect. And I have just the thing for your hair." She smiled over her shoulder and disappeared into the bathroom.

What summer dress? It was winter when I came here the first time. I finished feeding Airy and then carried her with me into the bedroom. I placed her on the floor and opened the closet. A pale sleeveless dress the color of sage hung there. There were several layers to the skirt, each hemline different and off-centered. It reminded me of something from the roaring twenties with its straight lines and simple but unusual design. I never would have bought this dress, but it was perfect for a wedding, the color just right to go with my red hair. As far as shoes, I wouldn't wear any. I picked up the paper where I'd scribbled my vows the night before, looking it over. I would never remember all this! Should I shorten it or take the paper along and read it?

∽

"Maeve!" I heard my mother call. I picked up the baby who had found the egg carton under the bed and was playing with it. I grabbed it away from her and stashed it in the dresser drawer. I'd pulled hair from Harold's comb, mixing it with my saliva, and placed it there weeks ago. I'd forgotten all about it.

"Coming!" I called, heading into the other room.

Finna held out a circlet of gold with a Celtic knot symbol on the front. "For your hair."

"It's beautiful! Where did it come from?"

"Catriona wore it the day she and Eron—"

"But I thought they never got married."

Finna smirked. "They didn't. From what your grandmother told me it was very similar to what you're about to do—and not legally binding."

I laughed. "Will we jump over a broomstick?"

"The hand fasting is what I'd thought. I have the ribbons."

"And where did that dress come from? I've never seen it before in my life."

Finna looked puzzled. "It isn't yours?"

"No, Mum. I came in winter, remember?"

"Well then, the faery's must have brought it."

I pondered that. It did look like a faery dress, but at this moment I didn't feel very cordial towards them. "Which faeries? Surely not the Tel-quessir, and it couldn't have been the Sluagh or the Gwyllion."

"Perhaps it was the Bwbachod. They're household faeries and it's just the sort of thing they like to do." She laughed. "But you'd better make sure you and Harold drink champagne later—they hate it when humans don't consume alcohol."

The sun was sinking into the western sea when Harold and I took our places on the cool sand. My feet were bare, my windblown tangle kept in place with the circlet of gold. Harold's dark hair was pulled back and tied with a strip of leather. He wore a white linen shirt over his clean jeans, his feet bare as well. Gathered around us were Mum, holding Airy, and Dad, Eron, Duncan, Oak, Rea, and a few other Crion, two wildmen who's names escaped me, and Tannith, Dougal and Iain and of course everyone's spouses and babies. I thought I saw our old friends, Mikdal and Herska, in the shadows, and hoped I was right. I hadn't seen them since the war ended; Harold had yet to thank the older man properly for giving him Argyll. My creature of magic, Pooka, was standing just outside the circle, as though one of the guests. His golden eyes met mine for a moment and I thought I saw an expression of approval there.

MacCuill was officiating, wearing his white ceremonial robes, his deep blue eyes glittering in the dusky light. He had bound our hands together with the silk ribbon that matched my dress, and now Harold and I faced one another waiting for the druid to tell us what our next task might be.

"Which one will begin the vows?" he asked.

I stared at Harold, realizing that I no longer had access to my paper, and from the look on his face he'd just realized the same thing for himself.

"I will," he said, seeming to arrive at a decision. Our eyes met. "I come to you humbly," he said, "leaving the hurts of the past behind. You are my heart, Maeve, my soul mate, the one I hope to spend the rest of my life with. It doesn't matter where we are. All that matters is that we're together. I pledge my troth to you and promise to never lie."

I giggled when I heard the 'pledge my troth' bit, but a moment later I had to wipe tears from my eyes. I took a breath and began mine. "I love you, Harold, and I will always. You are my best friend, my lover and the father of my child. No matter what pulls us apart we will always find each other again, as evidenced by these past months. I give myself to you freely and without reservation."

We gazed at each other for several long moments after this, some unseen force moving between us. In my mind I saw some winged gossamer creature weaving a delicate ribbon around the two of us. Perhaps it was some part of the Fae who had come to pay their respects, or perhaps it was only my imagination. Whatever it was, Harold felt it too, his widened eyes registering his surprise.

A moment later MacCuill unwrapped the ribbon from around our hands. "You are officially husband and wife," he said, smiling widely.

A moment later Harold grabbed my hand and pulled me to face him. He stared at me with an expression of love that nearly brought tears to my eyes before lifting my left hand and slipping a ring onto my fourth finger. I gazed down at the Celtic knot design—the beautiful gold band that felt as though I'd always worn it. "It this what you and Dad were doing today?"

"I ordered it two months ago, before we'd even decided to have the ceremony."

"Harold, you may kiss the bride," I heard MacCuill say.

Harold took me in his arms, his mouth meeting mine in a kiss too passionate to be seen by anyone other than the people gathered here. As soon as we pulled apart a cheer went up, everyone clapping, whistling and yelling congratulations.

Our eyes met often as we received the individual congratulations and laughed and talked with people we hadn't seen in a long while. "Did we really do this?" Harold whispered at one point, and when I smiled he grabbed me round the waist and twirled me. Airy toddled among the guests and I saw other babies close to her age toddling with her. I heard flute music and drums in the distance and realized that a band of sorts was starting up.

Harold and I moved apart after that and I saw him carry his sword to Dougal and present him with it. To me this was a strong symbol of his commitment—Kenneth's sword would now be taken back into Otherworld where it belonged.

It was later, after we'd made the rounds and were standing together again, that Finna brought over two flutes of champagne, her eyes alight with happiness. "Lovely vows," she whispered, "and the binding—well, that last bit was unexpected."

I opened my mouth to say something but she was already hurrying away to pass out more champagne. Harold looped his arm through mine before we took our first sip. "Mo ghaol ort," he whispered.

The Gaelic words caught me by surprise. They meant 'my love is with you', but I wouldn't have expected Harold to say them. I pulled back to look at him, but he only waggled his eyebrows and grinned.

Coming soon:

Time Gap—what happens when past and present collide?

Other books by Nikki:

Moonstone--Wolfmoon Book I (formerly: The Moonstone)
Willow—Wolfmoon Book II (formerly: Saille, the Willow)
Raven—Wolfmoon Book III (formerly: The Wolf Moon)

The Bridge—can a shared destiny travel across time?
(formerly: The Bridge of Mist and Fog)

Gypsy's Quest--a time travel romance
Gypsy's Return—a time travel romance
Gypsy's Secret—a time travel romance

Just Another Desert Sunset
Coyote Sunrise

The Wolf Moon—a supernatural fantasy (re-do of Willow and
Raven)

Murder in Plain Sight—Book 1 Summer McCloud
paranormal mystery series
Saffron and Seaweed—Book 2 Summer McCloud
paranormal mystery series
Black and White and Red all Over—Book 3 Summer
McCloud paranormal mystery series

www.nikkibroadwell.com